Dead Quiet

Dead Quiet

Ian Aspley

Matador
Unit E2 Airfield Business Park,
Harrison Road, Market Harborough,
Leicestershire. LE16 7UL
Tel: 0116 2792299
Email: books@troubador.co.uk
Web: www.troubador.co.uk/matador
Twitter: @matadorbooks

ISBN 978 1803131 948

British Library Cataloguing in Publication Data.
A catalogue record for this book is available from the British Library.

Printed and bound in the UK by TJ Books LTD, Padstow, Cornwall
Typeset in 10.5pt Adobe Garamond Pro by Troubador Publishing Ltd, Leicester, UK

Matador is an imprint of Troubador Publishing Ltd

To Karen who has believed in my work and in me.
With all my heart I'd like to say thank you.

Chapter 1

The grey clouds raced in front of a full moon. But the cold November sky was being pelted by a stream of multicoloured fireworks. Two exited children with their parents stood open mouthed pointing up towards the darkened sky watching it being painted red then green. Another then another. The air was being chocked by the smoke and the smell of gun powder. But the old lady taking her dog for a walk, didn't give them a second glance. But she hoped they would pass over soon. Her dog growled as two drunken youths staggered past her talking loosely about the attractive new barmaid in the "CAT AND MOUSE" public house just up the road. She stood and watched them disappear down High Street. She had no choice her dog had just decided to cock it's leg up a dimly lit streetlight. Walking on again, she turned off the busier street then turned into a narrow alleyway which took her away from the noisy pubs and clubs. Eventually it would take her through the cemetery and back home. Once out of the alleyway, she strolled past several locked-up garages and boarded up shops that was awaiting to be demolished. Wire meshed fencing protected its surroundings from anymore mindless vandalism. It was once a thriving little street. Until a big supermarket chain was built which saw to that. Not a soul was about. The street was deserted. Only the street lights that lined the road would keep her company. The tall bare branched trees started to creak and sway in a rising wind. She had walked this street many times before. How many times. She would not like to say. But as more fireworks illuminated the sky, she had an uneasy feeling about tonight. For some reason she had the worrying sense that she was being followed. She thought she could hear a set of footsteps echoing behind her. Suddenly she stopped dead in her tracks, then turned up her fake fur collar from the biting wind. She slowly half turned, but nobody was there. She rolled her eyes as she looked down at her whimpering dog. She started to walk off again until she noticed a young boy of about fifteen sheltering in an empty shop doorway trying to keep out the nighttime chill. As she got nearer to him. On the ground next to him lay a stuffed Guy Fawkes. The teenager started to ring out in song

"Remember, remember the fifth of November, gunpowder, treason and plot, penny for the Guy Mrs?" he said holding out his hand as she was about to walk past.

"No thank you" she said hurrying past him.

"Miserable cow" he muttered under his breath.

Finally, she had reached the churchyard. She sighed deeply into the air as she opened the squeaky metal gate. She walked through it making the gate clang shut noisily behind her. The church stood on her left which had weathered over time. Centuries of harsh weather had beaten hard against it. It still stood proud and tall in the shimmering moon light with the hint of the odd colour of fireworks exploding behind it. The dog stopped to sniff its surroundings making the woman stop in her tracks again. She frowned as she looked over in the distance to her left. In the shades of the dim orange lamp glow, she noticed what looked like another Guy Fawkes. But this one didn't seem to have an owner! This one was slumped up against a headstone dressed in shabby clothes. She wondered over to it. She screamed only the once, but it was enough to get the attention of two teenage girls heading home from a night out further up the street. After running towards the woman. The girls found her sobbing uncontrollably on the ground next to her dog. Her hands clenched tight up against her face. One of the teenagers looked down at the slumped figure. Gasping, she immediately dialed the emergency number.

"They're on their way, it will be a couple of minutes before they arrive" said the young girl putting her phone back into her shoulder bag.

On hearing that, the old lady continued to cry and shaking her head in panic.

"I must get home; my husband will be worrying where I am" she spluttered.

"Everything's going to be ok" said the other young girl putting her arm around her.

The full moon appeared from behind the racing clouds. Shedding light on the three huddled figures now standing in the churches doorway. In the distance the wind carried the sound of sirens from a nearby street. A couple of long minutes later, and the approach of a panda car screeched to a halt lighting up everything blue in its wake. One of the uniformed officers alighted from his panda car armed with a torch and straightening his cap as he slammed his car door shut whilst the other stayed in the warmth of the car radioing back to the station. He switched on his torch, and then headed up the dimly lit path finding the figures standing in the shadows waiting for him.

"What seems to be the trouble ladies?" he said shining his torch at them.

"There's a dead body lying beside that headstone" said one of the young girls pointing towards it.

"You sure it's not a guy Madam, it is the season for Guys?" he said patronizingly.

"Do you think this poor woman would be in this state if it was just a stuffed Guy?" said the other still hugging the woman. He walked over to the headstone in question still shining his torch. That is when he noticed the slumped figure lying in a fresh pool of blood. He fumbled for his radio on his lapel, then radioed back to his colleague still sitting in the warmth of the car.

"Alpha one, come in, over."

"Alpha one, what is it, don't tell me the old ladies scared of the dark?" he said through the static of his radio.

"No, it's more than that, we have a dead corpse on our hands."

At the end of a long tiring shift all that Detective Sergeant Karen Abbot wanted to do is put her feet up in front of the fire and maybe relax with a little light TV, and a nice glass of wine to finish off her day. By the time she got home, hopefully the children should be in bed asleep and her husband Richard would have made her something nice to eat. Nothing too fancy, as Richard didn't like "foreign mucked about stuff." His words not hers. Something along the lines of a cottage pie or cheese on toast. That was all about he could master anyway. But at least it would be hot and edible. Well, that was what she was hoping anyway. Hoping he had made something, at least especially with things being frosty in the air between the two of them lately. Just then her

4

office desk phone rang interrupting her from her thoughts. She rolled her eyes, as she glanced at her wristwatch. Should she answer it or leave it to ring?

Chapter 2

Karen Abbot was a stunner. She was in her early fifties with shoulder length brown hair, slim build, and deep brown eyes with high cheek bones to match. Her skin as smooth as a peach. Smoothing down her red knee length skirt she checked on her makeup in her small vanity mirror she just got out from her top desk draw. Just then her door knocked loudly.

"Come in" she shouted.

The door flung wide open, and Sergeant Ian Peter's poked his head around it. Sergeant Ian Peter's was Abbots former colleague. He'd been working with her on and off for a number of years now ever since she arrived in uniform from her old station. Her old station had been in Greenock, about eight miles out of Glasgow. But that had to close down due to lack of resources. Which really didn't help matters due to the increase in crime there. Abbot got despondent with matters in Scotland. That's why she headed for a new beginning here. Ryde police station on the Isle of Wight.

As a Scottish newcomer she fitted in really well. She quickly got promoted through the ranks. A little to quickly for some long-serving officers in the force who held a slight grudge. Rumours around the station joked that they might have slept together at some point in their career. But her only regret was that the hours were not nine to five as was in Scotland. Abbot liked the sound of a slower pace of life. Hence her move to the island. But she soon realised after moving here she'd be working even longer hours by picking up the pieces of holiday makers drunken behaviour. Richard her husband didn't want to move. He liked it where he was. It had been a difficult decision for them both. Working as a rep for a pharmaceutical company called neurotec, Richard could easily be transferred to their Portsmouth office. So, ferrying across on the hovercraft each day made it relatively easy. They also had a six year old daughter at the time of moving, but to Sophie it had all been a big adventure. A new school. Making new friends. All so innocent for a six-year-old. Soon Sergeant Ian Peter's will have bigger fish to fry. He'd just been promoted to drug squad on the mainland and would be working with the Hampshire police force. Working with the big boys trying to solve bigger related crimes. The timing of the move for Peter's was still up in the air for him. He could be here another week, or it could be as long as six months depending on if there were any transfer placements. Sergeant Peter's was a quite handsome middleman, single forty-eight-year-old and living in rented accommodation in a B&B near to Cowes on the other side of the island. He had deep ocean blue eyes and was always dressed immaculately whilst his light brown hair never seemed to be ever out of place.

"Ah, sit down Peters."

"Ehh, I didn't come in to sit down, I came in to tell you" he said moving completely into the room now.

"Tell me what Peters, can't it wait, I'm just about to go home?" she said interrupting him glancing at her wristwatch again.

"Please don't laugh when I tell you" he said scratching his forehead.

"You haven't told me anything yet, get on with it, I haven't got all night" she said in frustration. "Ok, don't say I didn't warn you."

"Oh, get on with it, would you"

"A young girls just phoned in to say that they've found a dead man up in Yarmouth cemetery, she thought it was a stuffed Guy at first, I did try phoning you, but your office phone just kept ringing out" he said putting his hands in his pockets.

"Ehh, I must have been in the middle of something Sergeant" she said responding quickly but unable to make eye contact. She rolled her eyes as she put her vanity mirror back into her desk draw then brushed down her skirt again.

"A dead man in the cemetery" she said frowning.

"Yeah."

"What's it got to do with me anyway?"

"We've been asked by the Chief Constable upstairs to go and have a look" he said pointing towards the ceiling.

"Oh, you've got to be kidding me, does he know I'm off home in ten minutes?" she said irritatedly.

"I told him that, but he seems to think."

"Anyway, you're not even on my team now, where's my new Sergeant, Sergeant Jones, or whatever his name is?" she said interrupting him again.

"He went home not ten minutes ago, he told me to tell you he'll see you in the morning so, it looks like just you and me tonight then" he said smiling.

"Ain't I the lucky one" she said sighing.

"Umm" he said distantly.

"You see Peter's, this is why I don't answer my phone when I'm just about to end my shift" she said rolling her eyes at him.

"Ok, I'll have to try that" he muttered in weak agreement.

A few moments later and they were driving west of the island down dark winding eery narrow lanes with low hedges either side. The piercing light from The Needle's Lighthouse rotated slowly in front of them. In the distance blue lights flickered. Their bodies lurched into their seats as Abbot pressed her foot hard on the accelerator making the car weave in and out of the white lines in the middle of the road swerving past a one-way street causing them to both pray nothing was coming the other way. They finally arrived at the crime scene. Peter's knuckles were white from holding on tight on his passenger's seat. She parked her silver Volvo next to the patrol car that was blocking the cemetery gates. The area had been sealed off by police tape and a crowd of onlookers had formed from the nearby pubs and clubs speculating what may have happened. Both detectives eventually alighted from the car. Abbot pulled up her coat collar up above her ears to try and keep out the night time chill. The biting wind whistled around them both as they approached the Constable standing keeping guard. Abbot waved her warrant card at him. He nodded slightly then let the two detective's past. They walked the few hundred paces up the path to where the other constable stood with his torch still shining.

"Ok Constable, what we got here?" she asked looking down at the body.

"Ehh, a dead tramp ma'am, looks like he was drunk, then fell up against this headstone."

"Umm, you could be right, but there's an awful lot of blood from a fall wouldn't you say Constable?"

"Ma'am."

"Who found the body?" she said flipping strands of windswept hair behind her left ear. The Constable pointed towards the three figures where the old lady was still being consoled by the teenager still inside the church doorway.

"The lady with the dog ma'am, just waiting on a statement, she's very upset, I couldn't get anything out of her."

"I bet she's, not as upset as I am Constable, I should have been home ages ago?" she said putting her cold hands into her coat pockets.

"Sorry Ma'am, that's exactly what the old lady keeps saying" he said shivering.

"Go on Constable, you go and sit in your car and get warm, it's freezing out here, I'll deal with this."

"Thank you, Ma'am," he said walking off in the direction of his panda car.

"Oh Constable, before you go, pass me your torch, would you?" she shouted holding out her hand.

He turned back and handed it over to her with a reassuring smile. She thanked him then looked back at Peter's.

"Sergeant, can you get a statement from the old lady, and the two girls, find out if they saw anything out of the ordinary, oh, and keep it brief, I want to get home tonight, I'll give the body a wee quick look over?" she said walking around the body.

She shone the torch from head to toe along the body, and from a quick inspection she noticed that the dead man had blood clotted in his hair and on his clothes. He looked around the age of sixty five, and there were no obvious signs of cuts to his hands. So, no sign of a struggle and no sharp weapons out of the ordinary lay near or around his body.

10

Then after a couple of long minutes Peter's wondered back over to her.

"Got anything?" he asked curiously putting his hands in his coat pockets.

"He's a tramp alright, poor sod, and there's no pulse."

"Could he have been drunk, fell over and hit his head like the constable said?" he asked frowning.

"No, there's far too much blood for a fall, plus his coats full of blood" she said switching off the torch.

"His own?" he asked curiously.

"Looks that way" she said with a sigh.

"Ehh Mrs Dawkins wants to know if she can go home now, she said her husband will be wondering where she is, as she's never out this late?" he said looking back over at the old lady in the distance.

"I know how she feels, oh, did you get a brief statement?"

"I had done just as you asked" he said smiling to himself.

"Ok, tell her she can go."

"Oh, and what about the two girls as well, and yes, I've got their brief statements too?"

"Thank you, Sargeant," she said softly.

"I did say, we might have to contact them again, you know, if we ever need to" he said cutting himself off shivering.

"Where's Soco, they should be here by now?" she asked as he was about to walk away.

"They're on route, they got stuck in the roadworks on the Yarmouth Road, they just radioed in."

Just then in the distance she saw the duty Doctor pull up alongside her car. He climbed out then reached for his briefcase off the backseat, slamming his door shut then pushed aside two bystanders blocking his way.

He walked briskly up the footpath to where the two detectives stood waiting impatiently for him.

"Well, well, Abbot what do we have here then, we don't get many murders on the Isle of Wight, I thought you'd be at home with your feet up by the fireside, I wasn't expecting to see you here tonight?" he said clutching his briefcase.

"Well sorry to disappoint you doc, but I wasn't expecting to see you either?" she said despondently.

The Doctor put down his briefcase next to the body then opened it getting out a pair of blue latex gloves and his thermometer. Abbot rolled her eyes at Peter's discreetly as the doctor put on the gloves.

"What's wrong doc, you never examined a dead tramp before?"

"Come to think of it, I've never examined a live one before" he said moving in closer to the body.

"Well, we all have to make sacrifices somewhere doc, unfortunately, mines not going home to a nice meal, and two adorable children, oh, and not forgetting the glass of wine" she said jovially.

"And what about Richard?" he asked curiously moving the body slightly onto its side.

"Oh, and him as well" she said as an afterthought.

The church clock chimed the half hour. She glanced at her wristwatch. Half past midnight on a freezing cold Friday night. She shouldn't even be here. This should be night duties problem.

As if she did not have enough problems already. She'd had another argument with Richard two nights previous.

This had been happening a lot lately. She'd promised him that she'd try and work less hours. If not for him, then for the girls."

They'd both met each other at a 'RunRig' concert at the Barrowlands in Glasgow. They found they shared the same taste in music, following their idols and going to concerts together whenever they could make the time. Maybe Sterling castle or even Edinburgh castle.

Ever since the move, it seemed to have affected almost everything and now maybe their marriage.

Maybe that's why she was subconsciously working longer hours, so she didn't have to go home to arguments.

The doctor had finished his examination.

"Looks like he's been hit over the head with a very heavy instrument" he said standing back up.

"Any idea with what doctor?" inquired Peter's.

"I should know more when I do the postmortem, it's hard to see anything in this light but he'd have died in minutes, looking at these injuries, I should know by the end of tomorrow morning" he said taking of his rubber gloves.

"Ok doctor" said Peter's nodding slightly.

"It could have been a hammer or a cosh, something heavy anyway" he added closing up his briefcase.

"Anything in his pocket's doc?" she asked glancing over at Peter's.

"No, there's nothing in his pockets at all to indicate who he is, I'm afraid Sergeant."

"Can you tell if there's any other injuries doc?" she asked curiously.

"Like I said, Abbot, I'll have a good look at him properly once I get him back to the lab, I can't say fairer than that now, can I?"

"Time of death?" she asked.

"Ohh, not long, half hour, maybe an hour at most, by the temperature of his body, not very long at all."

"Ok, thanks doc" she said moving away from him.

"I'll send you my report sometime tomorrow Abbot, good night" he shouted halfway down the path.

Just as the Doctor pulled away in his car, a white transit van took its place. It was the Soco team at last.

"Where you lot been, we've been waiting ages?" growled Peter's as the team approached him.

"Sorry Sir we got…" said one of the men cutting himself off.

"Yes, ok, stuck in roadworks, your here now, he's over there by that gravestone" he said pointing towards it.

A couple of minutes later, Abbot and Peter's started to walk slowly back towards her car.

"So, what are you thinking?" he asked frowning.

"Oh, I don't know Sergeant, this job can be so blooming unpredictable sometimes."

"Meaning?"

They stopped as they reached the cemetery gate instead of walking through it. Then, half turned back to look at the activity of the SOCO's. A couple from the team was still fetching floodlights from the back of their vehicles.

The majority of the crowd had dispersed now making their way back to the warmth of the pubs and clubs.

"Oh, I don't know Sergeant" she said sighing leaning on the gate.

A couple of minutes later and they'd climbed into the car. She turned the key in the ignition to let some heat blow through from the heater vents. She stared blankly out of the car window looking up at the church clock.

"First, we have to find out who the dead man is?"

"Was" he said correcting her.

"Ok, was" she said sighing.

She leaned her head hard against the leather headrest and sighed again.

"So, I'm thinking, without any identification on the body it's going to be blooming impossible don't you think,

I mean who's going to miss a dead tramp, he's obviously got no immediate family to report him missing has he?"

Peter's crunched up his face.

"But our first priority Sergeant, is to find out who he is, or was and then after that the what, and the why?"

Peter's yawned.

"Once we've caught the killer or killers, we can then try to give, if he had any kind of family, some kind of closure."

"Yeah, they'll get twenty years, out in twelve, for good behaviour" he said disgustingly.

"Now he's dead, we're going to care more about him now, than when he was alive, seems wrong doesn't it?" she said looking over at Peter's.

He smiled at her briefly.

"Like I said Sergeant, so blooming unpredictable."

She clipped her seatbelt into the holder then engaged the car into gear then drove off into the darkness.

Chapter 3

Early the following morning Abbot walked through the lobby door just by the front desk looking a bit worse for wear.

The WPC on the front desk was stirring her hot cup of tea with the end of her pen.

"Oh, ma'am a message from Chief Constable Green, he wants to see you urgently."

"What now, I've just walked in can't he wait?"

"Urgent, he said, soon as you walk through that door" she said taking a sip of her hot tea.

"Oh right, I'd better not disappoint him then, had I?" she said punching her four digit number into
the security door.

She finally reached the Chief Constables office from down the warren of narrow corridors and gave the door a light tap. She waited for a long second.

"Come in" was heard coming from behind it.

She slowly opened the door then walked in closing it behind her. The Chief Constable sat behind his large oak desk, leaning back in his chair.

"You wanted to see me Sir?" she said jovial.

"Ahh Abbot, take a seat, will you."

He was a tall stocky man of about sixty, with grey reseeding hair and a goaty beard. She collected a chair from near to the window then placed it opposite his desk.

"Glad you're in early, I wanted a word with you about this cemetery murder business."

"Oh, that's not my case Sir, I only went there last night because no one else was available to go" she said correcting him quickly.

"I want you in charge of this case Abbot?" he said leaning forward in his chair.

"With all due respect Sir, I'm already on a case."

"Which one?" he asked frowning.

"The three house burglaries, I think I'm getting closer to catching the perpetrators Sir" she said flipping her hair behind her left ear.

"Give it to someone else?" he said sighing loudly.

"Like whom, Sir?" she asked curiously frowning.

"I don't know Abbot, look you're an experienced detective, you shouldn't be doing bottom of the pile cases. I want you in charge of this case, but I want it done by the book" he said pointing at her with his index finger.

"But Sir?"

"No butts, I want you in charge, give yourself to prove yourself."

"I do prove myself Sir, I'm quite proud of my arrest rate" she said confidently.

"Yes, well, don't overdo it Abbot, pride becomes before a fall as they say."

"Who does Sir?"

"Well, I don't know do I, it's a saying, oh never mind?" he said shaking his head in frustration at her.

"I won't let you down Sir" she said all excited.

"Let's hope not Abbot, I've got no worries about you, that's why I want you in charge?"

"But who shall I give my case load too then Sir?"

"Oh, I don't know, what about Jones, he should be taking it easy anyway at his time of life?"

"Ok right Sir."

"I want Peter's working with you on this one Abbot, he won't be here much longer, I don't think, you two get on well and you both works hard".

"Is there a replacement come up for him then Sir?" she asked holding his stare.

"Umm, there just might be."

"Sir" she said with a forced smile.

"You don't have to worry; I'll back you up all the way if you need anything and it's in my power, I'll do my best to get it for you."

"Thank you, Sir."

"Your one of my finest detectives Abbot, although your Scottish."

They both laughed heartily.

"But we won't hold that against you but keep me informed."

"Thank you again Sir." she said proudly still smiling.

She rose to her feet then put the chair back from where she found it. Then she brushed down her skirt as she headed for the door.

Later that morning, in the briefing room, the air was thick with plumes of cigarette smoke. Sounds of loud chatter, and distant coughing came from the far corner of the room.

A handful of detectives had been drafted in from other divisions that had to be briefed about last night's incident. She wondered into the middle of the room to introduce herself coughing into her fist.

"Ok good morning everyone, my name is Detective Sergeant Karen Abbot, for those who don't know me, and I know some of you who have worked with me before, so, I've just been put in charge of this case, I don't know if any of you are aware of what happened last night in Yarmouth cemetery?" she said smiling.

A few mumbles echoed the room.

"Ok, at around 10pm last night, we had a call to say that an old man may have fallen over and knocked himself unconscious, but on arrival, myself and Sergeant Peter's didn't find him unconscious, we found him dead, slumped up against a gravestone, so we are treating this as a murder inquiry as from now, I apologise for being a wee bit grumpy this morning, I'm not always like this, but I've had very wee sleep last night as I'm sure Sergeant Peter's will tell you."

The room echoed with loud wolf whistles and laughter. She rolled her eyes raised and her right hand.

"Any more of that, and you all will be demoted to lollipop duties, do I make myself clear?" she said firmly.

The room hushed into a quiet silence. She turned around then walked over to a white board that stood in the middle of the room. On it she stuck several coloured A4 sized photos. Looking back at her was the man in his late sixties, with grey hair, and a grey beard, with a very weathered looking face. Two other photos showed the man's head injuries.

"Ok everybody listen up, this is our man, I had these photos taken before his postmortem, we have no name, and no fixed address as yet, so whoever is he, and where has he been residing, It's November, it's freezing out there, so where's all his belongings, we didn't find any at, or near the scene, so somebody must know where they are, or better still, have they got them or dumped them somewhere, or knows of someone who has?" she said looking at the photos.

She moved over to the middle of the room again, then sat on the edge of an unoccupied desk then folded her arms.

"We found nothing in his pockets, no kind of identification, or anything else for that matter, so it's going to make this investigation a wee bit harder than usual."

"Why's that then ma'am?" someone asked from the back of the room.

"Because no one has reported him missing, as I've already said, we don't even have a name, so we need to find out about his last known movements" she said half turning to face the group.

She unfolded her arms then wondered back over to the whiteboard. She fumbled through a mixture of coloured dry marker pens then picked up the black one. She popped off the top then started to scribble down words on it.

"Was he with anyone?"

"Was he alone when he fell?"

"Was it a mugging gone wrong ma'am?" asked another detective from the back of the room.

She stepped back from the board again for a long second.

"If so, why would you want to mug a tramp detective?" she asked waiting for his name.

"Detective Smith ma'am."

"Detective Smith?" she repeated.

The detective rolled his eyes at her from behind his computer screen as she looked back at the whiteboard.

"For one thing, he wouldn't be wearing any expensive jewellery, or have any amount of cash on him, would he?"

She looked around the room at the detectives' blank faces.

"No, this must have been a personal attack, did someone hold a grudge against him, I want the person or persons responsible caught?"

She paused for a long second, putting the dry marker up to her lips.

"Who wanted him dead, and why, our main priority is to find out who this man was, and then why he was attacked, he might be a vagrant, but he is still a human being, he's still someone's son?"

Another shout from the back of the room.

"Do we know the circumstances of what happened yet ma'am?"

"Very little as yet constable Hyde, but if you were paying any attention, you would have known" she said rolling her eyes at him.

Loud heckles came from the room.

"All we know as yet is that he had a very nasty blow to the back of his head, implement unknown, but the doc may think it maybe a hammer or a cosh, of some kind?" she said flipping her hair behind her left ear.

"Hopefully, the postmortem will shed some light on what the object was when we get it back later today, also I want a team of you to go and check any CCTV in and around the area where he was attacked, also check the local pubs and clubs, see if anybody saw him in any of them or knows who he is, that doesn't give you the excuse to have a pint whilst you're on duty."

The room broke out in laughter once again.

"Also, go in the local shops and ask if they've seen him walking around the streets begging, show them his photo you have in front of you, and ask if they had to move him on?"

She replaced the marker pen into its holder then rubbed her hands together.

"Ok everyone, thank you for your time and argue amongst yourselves who's working with who boys and girls, come on chop chop" she said clapping her hands.

Loud mumbles came from the back of the room. Just then her mobile phone rang. She looked at the caller ID" school?"

"Hello."

"Yes, but."

"You're kidding me."

"What now, but I'm in a very important briefing, can't it wait?"

"Alright, I'll be there in half an hour" she said pressing the end call button.

She beckoned Peter's over from delegating detectives into groups.

"What's the matter?" he said walking sideways to get through the crowd of detectives.

"I have to pop out for a while, could you take over here for me?"

"What is it?" he asked curiously putting his hands on his hips.

"I've got to go and explain to my daughter's Headmistress why she hasn't bothered doing her homework again" she said rolling her eyes.

They both left the briefing room then walked quickly down the narrow corridor. Down through the double doors then turned left that lead to the front desk.

"Oh, I could kill her."

"Your daughter or the Headmistress?"

"Headmistresses, she's got one of those faces you want to slap" she said angrily.

They reached the security door then walked out into the foyer area. Peters stood by the security door. She stopped in her tracks then turned back towards Peter's. Then gave him a smile.

"Thanks for covering for me, I'll be as quick as I can, I have my phone on me, so if there's any developments call me, but I've put it on silent, so leave a message?" she said smiling at him.

"You carry on, we've got it covered here."

"You're a star, I owe you one" she shouted from across the car park.

"You owe me more than one?" he shouted, but by this time she was out of earshot and getting into her car.

Chapter 4

As she approached the school car park. It was overflowing with teachers' cars. Tutting, she put the car into reverse, and reversed back out the car park and onto the main road.

She could only find a space on the yellow hatched lines, where it read "STRICTLY NO PARKING."

She alighted her car slamming the door shut as she headed towards the main entrance. She went through numerous doors and down long narrow corridors.

"This place is like a rabbit hole; now where do I go?" she thought to herself coming to what looked like a dead end.

She turned back on herself then started to walk the way she'd just came from. On the left of her was rows and rows of cloak hangers filled with coats and rucksacks with names written in black ink on stickers. She never noticed them the first time.

Above the coats and rucksacks painted pictures from various children of all ages lined the various shades of cream and brown walls. Eventually, she found the Headmistress' office and was met by the acting principle.

"Can I help you Madam?" she said in a posh soft voice.

"Hello yes I'm Sophie Abbots Mum."

"Ah yes I'll tell the Headmistress you are here, if you wouldn't mind waiting in here, she won't be long" said the woman opening the headmistress's office door.

Abbot walked in and sat down on a child-size plastic chair near to the desk. The room smelt of beeswax and furniture polish. Above the desk on the walls hung numerous black and white pictures of old school years.

A few minutes later the office door flung wide open, and Abbot was greeted by a large passive woman. Big breasted, with long grey hair and around her neck, a pair of black spectacles that hung on a chain.

She pulled her cardigan closer around her large bosom and sat down at her well-polished desk. The woman reminded Abbot of an old spinster lady who has never been showed any love and not been able to give any back in all probability.

"Well, where do we start Mrs Abbot, your daughter has yet again, not handed in her homework project, what do you say to that?"

Abbot's mouth opened, but nothing came out. She was interrupted before she could get her words out.

"Three letters?" the indignant woman exclaimed.

"Three letters have been sent out to you in the post, and there's still no improvement, do you realise the seriousness Mrs Abbot?"

The Headmistress didn't wait for a reply.

"I'm afraid I'm going to have to give your daughter detention, detention I tell you" she repeated angrily.

"Yes but" she tried saying.

Abbot was spoken over yet again.

"No use trying to tell me she doesn't have any, because she has some to do every night of the week, and the last time she bought in any kind of homework, she got someone else in her class to do it all for her, is everything I've told you quite clear Mrs Abbot?" she said clasping her hands together.

Abbot stood up quickly from her chair. She looked straight at the headmistress and leaned against her desk.

"Don't you ever talk to me again like I'm one of your pupils, I'm in the middle of a murder inquiry, and you send me here on a wild goose chase to see where my daughter's poxy homework is, if I didn't have anything else better to do today, I would charge you with wasting police time, is that quite clear to you Miss Stick?"

She walked over to the door then half opened it turning back to look at the Headmistress still sitting gobsmacked at her desk.

"Oh, I see now why Sophie said it's like watching paint dry in your classes" she said slamming the door causing the papers on the impeccably smart desk to flutter onto the floor.

When Abbot reached her car. She noticed a parking ticket under her windscreen wiper. She ripped it off in disgust throwing it onto the back seat.

Back at the station Abbot felt tired and aching. She leaned back into her high-backed chair and raised both arms behind her head.

She thought about the regular arguments with Richard of late.

Sophie's schoolwork. This new murder case. All these things were playing on her mind. She sat back upright, then walked over to the door. shouting "Peter's" He glanced up at her from his computer screen.

"You and I are going on a jolly wee outing" she said putting her shoulder bag over her left shoulder.

"Oh, anywhere nice?" he asked dryly.

"Yes, the mortuary."

"Can't you phone them boss, them kinda places freak me out?" he said crunching up his face.

"Call yourself a copper, anyway, on the way you can tell me all about your love life, that will take your mind off things?" she said smiling opening the briefing room door.

"What love life, I haven't gone one?" he said smiling back.

"Exactly, you'll have to talk about the weather then instead, won't you?" she said sarcastically.

As they indicated right and pulled into the mortuary car park, every car space was taken. She spotted an empty space just over by the main entrance to the building. She sped up and drove straight into it.

"You're not going to…?" he said cutting himself off.

"Yes, and what is wrong with parking here, every other space is taken?" she said unhooking her seatbelt.

She turned off the ignition then alighted the car. Peter's shook his head in disbelief while he unhooked his seatbelt. After he alighted the car, he looked back to where they had parked still shaking his head.

"Yes, but there's a big sign on the wall that reads "NO PARKING AT ANYTIME.""

"Oh, forget that rubbish that's only for the general public" she said dismissing what he'd just said.

"What?" he gasped.

"Anyway, we're here in a different capacity" she said firmly as they walked through a set of double doors.

"I don't like this at all, if we're clamped when we...."

She stopped dead in her tracks and turned towards him.

"Oh, stop your moaning, it's only because you don't like these kinds of places, we're only going to be half an hour" she said walking off again.

After a short while walking in and out of various corridors. They finally found the pathologist lab.

On entry it smelt of strong sterilising fluids and disinfectant. On a table in the middle of the room were various strange shaped different sized looking implements.

"I told you I don't like these kinds of places" he said muttering under his breath.

"Stop your whining will you or else I will use one of them sharp implements on your.......ahh doc."

She said gritting her teeth.

She noticed the Doctor looking in their direction. In response he popped his head from around his office door.

"Ahh detectives, and what do I owe this pleasure, but you could have phoned, and I would have saved you the bother of coming all this way?" he said jovially.

"I told her to doctor but, she insisted on coming" he said looking at Abbot sideways.

"How lovely anyway" continued the pathologist who obviously didn't get the chance to chat to a lot of people in his line of work.

"Do we know how the victim was killed yet doc?" asked Abbot quickly.

"Well Abbot, the blow to the back of his head that killed him outright, we call that blood force trauma."

Abbot rolled her eyes at Peter's.

"But with the force of the blow, it cracked his skull open like an egg, if you find me the murder weapon, then I can match it up against the wound?" he added dryly.

"That narrows things down doc, thank you, I'll bear that in mind" she said rolling her eyes at Peter's again.

"There is one more interesting thing to note Abbot" he said raising his forefinger.

"What's that then doc, I didn't come here to play the guessing game?" she grumbled.

"Ok, I'll tell you."

"I wish you would doc" she said impatiently.

"Very well, he also had a single stab wound to his heart" he announced proudly.

"What would be the bloody point in that Doctor, if he was already dead?" inquired Peter's frowning.

"To make sure he was dead Sergeant, why else, but whoever killed him would have had some considerable amount of blood on him?" he added smirking.

"So, in other words, doc, the killer would have been covered in the stuff?" she asked politely.

"Most definitely" he said nodding his head in agreement.

"But the town was busy last night, someone must have seen him covered in blood surely?" she said raising her voice.

"To have that much blood on his clothing it would have been as though he bathed in it, I would have thought Abbot?" said the pathologist nodding his head again.

"Goodness as much as that, so how long would it take for the blood to start clotting before he was found doc?" she asked curiously.

"About half an hour at most, it was very cold last night, so it would have clotted that blood much quicker."

"So, not only have we got to find a heavy implement, but we've also now got to find a sharp bladed knife as well, great news that doc?" she said rolling her eyes.

She walked towards the door then pulled on the door handle.

"You'll be telling me next doc, that he was dead before he was even hit over the head or even stabbed?"

"Well. funny you should say."

Abbot made a hand gesture cutting him off in mid-sentence.

"Don't even go there doc, just fax me over your report when you've finished, would you?" she said opening the door.

When they reached Abbot's car a folded handwritten note in big black capital letters was under the driver's side windscreen wiper. She grabbed it then unfolded the note it read "CAN'T YOU READ?"

"I don't believe it, the cheek of some people" she said grumbling unlocking the car door.

She screwed it up and threw it on the back seat along with the other parking ticket she received earlier. Peter's looked on in amazement shaking his head.

"Oh, I think I need a coffee after that news don't you, Sergeant?" she said reversing out of the space.

"Watch that bollard!" he shouted grabbing hold of the dashboard.

"I can see it thank you" she yelled.

"I need more than a coffee with your parking and state of driving" he added.

She completely ignored his remark. She engaged the car into first gear then leapt her foot off the clutch speeding off screeching the tyres out of the car park. Making a passing cyclist manoeuvre awkwardly out her way just in time.

Chapter 5

That night Abbot took a detour home. Instead of going up by the roadworks past black gang chine and down the broadmean road. She decided to go for a drive along the Old Military Road which was on the north side of the island. She indicated left then pulled into the Isle of Wight Pearls car park.

She rolled down her window then lit a cigarette. For a couple of minutes, she sat looking out at the endless miles of Black Sea watching the relentless waves crashing hard against the eroding cliffs.

One after the other. Crashing and swirling.

In the far distance the famous lighthouse with its radiant bright light was cutting through the eerie dark night.

"That's how I feel about my life at the minute, just like the waves crashing and swirling with no kind of purpose." she muttered to herself blowing out a plume of smoke.

She tossed out the cigarette from her window as she drove back off into the darkness. She finally reached home then parked her car on the driveway not bothering to turn off the engine.

After a few long minutes she finally alighted the car then reached the front door. Her heart sank as she turned the key in the lock. She hesitantly walked through the front door with her key still in her hand.

On hearing the door slam shut Sophie came running out of her bedroom where her music was beating loudly. She stood at the top of the stairs and looked down over the bannister at her mum.

"Mum, can you take me to school tomorrow?"

"I thought dad was taking you?" she said shuffling out of her coat.

"Dad can't take me, he's got a meeting tomorrow, and he has to leave for work early" she shouted.

"Oh, your got to be kidding me" she said sighing as she put her coat on the bannister.

"Thanks mum."

"I'll see what I can do, but right now, I want a word with you young lady, about your homework" she said looking up at her.

"Mum, I don't need to do homework, I'm nearly sixteen, I'll be leaving school soon, anyway homework is for little children like Grace" she shouted down.

"Don't you talk about your sister like that, she's only eight" she said reprimanding the sullen teenager.

Sophie headed back into her bedroom in temper then slammed the door hard shut.

"Have you cleaned your room young lady?" she shouted over the loud music.

With no answer she tutted then shouted again.

"Sophie, can you turn that music down please, it sounds like a disco in here?"

She walked into the kitchen to find it full of mayhem. A disarray of dirty plates and dirty dishes that overflowed the sink and work tops. Faint repetitive booming came from the ceiling above her.

Sophie had only turned the music down a fraction. Abbot rolled her eyes at the ceiling.

Just then Grace came running in from the lounge. Nearly knocking Abbot over. Her face covered in chocolate.

"Grace, can you stop running in the kitchen please, where's daddy?" she asked turning off the water tap.

"He's in the other room reading" she said smiling up at her mum.

"Oh, is he" she said sighing.

Grace with a finger in her mouth went and stood next to her mum.

"What's the matter darling, sorry I didn't mean to shout, it's just been a long day that's all?" she said crouching down to her to wipe the chocolate off her face.

"Mummy, I saw daddy kissing Jacob's mummy in the playground today when he dropped me off at school" she said trying to push away from the wet cloth.

"Whose Jacob, darling?" she said trying to ignore the stabbing pain going through her chest as she concentrated on keeping her face set in a smile.

"Jacob Snow, mummy, he's in my class at school."

"I'll talk to daddy later about it alright darling, now you run along, there's a good girl" she said gripping the table edge as she stood up.

Her face was white under the forced smile. Her heart racing erratically.

"You just told me not to run in the kitchen mummy?" she said oblivious to her mummy's distress.

"I did didn't I darling, you're right as usual" she said leaning down again and gave her a kiss on her forehead.

Later, relaxing in the dimly lighted room on the sofa with a glass of white wine. Abbot asked Richard about kissing Graces friend's mum. He looked uncomfortable immediately.

"Oh that, she's found a new job and I was congratulating her, that's all" he said nervously.

"Oh yeah, where's she going then?" she asked taking a sip of wine, trying not to look nonchalant.

"She didn't say" he said looking away from her.

"But you kissed her anyway, a wee bit strange not to ask where her future employment is don't you think?" she said frowning.

"Fine I don't know alright, next time I see her I'll ask her for her shoe size, shall I?" he said spitting the words out.

"Don't be ridiculous, why does every conversation always end up in an argument, also Sophie tells me you can't take her to school tomorrow?" she said folding her arms tightly into her chest.

"Is that a crime now as well, is it?" he said sarcastically.

"Don't be so childish Richard."

"I'm not, and I rang you this morning telling you so about it, but your stupid phone went to answer machine, so I left you a message, obviously you didn't get it?" he added aggressively.

"What time this morning?"

"I'm not one of your suspects, Karen, I don't know, nine thirty or there about."

"Oh, forgive me Richard, but I was in a meeting about your daughters' homework, yet again, I put my phone on silent and forgot to change it back again, alright" she said tutting.

"No, it's not alright."

"I'll have to drop them off early on the way into work, then won't I, I just hope I don't get stuck in all that traffic where they got the road works, it's a nightmare there at the best of times?" she said unfolding her arms.

Richard got up from the sofa in frustration and walked over to the CD cabinet.

"Do you want to listen to a wee bit of Runrig?" he said looking through his CD collection.

"Sorry."

"We've got Heartlands, we've got Beat the drum, Long distance, Cutter and the clan?"

"Not tonight Richard, I may go and have a long relaxing soak and then get into bed, I'm beat."

"Fine, your upset and, I've got to suffer all night is that it?" he said putting a disk into the open slot.

"Do you have to Richard?"

"What, is it too loud?" he asked annoyed.

"No, just leave it, would you!"

"But you like Runrig?" he said sounding confused.

"You've made your point."

"What point Karen, if you've got a problem, let's talk about it?"

"Give it a rest, would you Richard."

"Fine, you're angry because I can't take the girls to school, fine, bloody fine!" he said pulling out another CD just to have something to do with his hands.

"It's not just that, I'm fed up with the arguments all the time, every time, we have a conversation it ends in one, like now" she said sighing.

"And?" he asked hesitantly.

"And I've been thinking, I think that we should have a break from each other for a while, just to see how things go?"

"What?" he said spitting the word out.

"Only for six months or so, I don't know how much longer I can take of it, it's just too much for me Richard" she said folding her leg up onto the sofa.

"Oh, so, I never consider any of your feelings now, is that it, great, just great?"

"I didn't say that, Richard."

"Fine" he said switching off the CD player.

He threw down the empty CD case he had in his hand onto the CD cabinet then huffed as he rushed out of the room slamming the door hard behind him.

"Is staying in the same room that bad now as well, is it?" she muttered under her breath.

That night Abbot couldn't sleep all she done was toss and turn. She looked at her alarm clock next to her bed, it read three twenty one am.

She looked back over at Richard lying there fast asleep. She couldn't help wondering why things had gone the way they had. Then she thought about their frequent arguments.

Their marriage, and the hours she was putting in at work lately. Her heart felt heavy. She got up, pulling back the curtains.

She looked out of the window. In the distance the corpses of trees swayed and swung in a rising wind. The full moon shone bright from behind the breaking clouds. Shivering, she drew back the curtains and got back into bed.

Chapter 6

She pulled up at the school gates at exactly eight thirty am. The traffic wasn't that bad considering. She smiled reassuringly at them both from her rear-view mirror. She turned in her seat to look at the girls.

"See, girls plenty of time."

"Oh, look Mummy, that's Jacobs Mummy over there" said Grace pointing excitedly over in the direction of the school playground.

Sophie had already alighted the car and was halfway through the school gates. She didn't want to be seen with her younger sister.

"Thank you Mummy" she said scrambling out the back door.

Abbot smiled and waved at her as she looked back and waved from the school gate.

"Love you, have a good day."

"Bye Mummy, love you" she shouted.

Just then she noticed Jacob's mum walking confidently across the school playground. Abbot watched her for a while. She had shoulder length blonde hair. Slim and very attractive. She looked familiar to Abbot. She couldn't help but watch the pretty woman. She walked through the school gates.

The woman got into the driver's side of a red sports car. Pushing her jealousy aside. Abbot managed to jot down the last three letters of the cars registration plate before the car disappeared out of view.

She was so busy scribbling down the number. She hadn't noticed Grace waving back at her.

She put the car into gear. And pulled off into the flow of slow-moving school traffic.

Later in her office whilst she'd got a quick five minutes. She phoned through to traffic division.

"Yes, hello this is DS Abbot from upstairs, could you do a vehicle check for me please?"

A long pause from the other end of the line.

"Yes, I'll hold" she said looking at the scribbled letters on a scrap piece of paper.

"Yes, ok it's…" she said relaying the registration number.

"Ok thank you very much, no no that's it thanks you" she said replacing the receiver into its cradle. Then she rose to her feet, then headed towards the door. She pulled down on the door handle, then walked into the outer office.

"Brrr it's freezing in here. It's probably warmer outside, can someone put the heating on?" she said rubbing her hands together.

"It is on" shouted Peter's as a hush fell on the room.

"Oh, right good job you and me are going out then, isn't it" she said looking at him.

"Where?" he asked frowning.

"Somewhere warmer, well, don't just sit there, get your coat."

"Not the mortuary again?" he said wearily putting on his coat.

"We're going back to the scene of crime, and on the way, you can tell me all about your love life, can't you?" she said smiling.

"You fancy me don't you, go on admit it?"

"Shut up Peter's, before I change my mind about the mortuary."

They both walked side by side down the corridor putting their hands on all the warm radiators. When they turned the corner, they noticed WPC Grange putting up a poster on the notice board.

"What's this then?" she asked frowning at the poster.

"It's Sergeant Jones's retiring doo Ma'am, didn't you know?" she said pulling at a piece of Blu-Tack.

"Didn't I know, didn't I, of course I didn't know, I thought he'd just started at this station, I don't know what you're laughing at Peter's, you don't have to work with him?" she growled.

Abbot started to read it out loud.

'You are all invited to the retirement of Ronnie Jones which will be held at the Wheat Sheaf Inn at Yarmouth, on the seventh of this month at eight pm. All are welcome, bring family and friends.'

"Ronnie, I've been calling him Charles!"

"I'm surprised he put 'all' are welcome, he should have said except for DS Abbot who can't get my name right!" he said shaking his head.

WPC Grange started laughing.

"Well, I'd like to go of course, but I don't have anyone to watch over the girls" said Abbot looking in Peter's direction.

"Don't look at me, I don't know what to do with kids?" he shrieked.

"You only have to watch one, the others sixteen and she can look after herself?"

"There you go, there's your answer" he said smirking.

"Come on, you haven't got anyone to take with you anyway, have you?"

"I'll go with you if you want a partner Sergeant?" said the WPC still pulling at a piece of Blu-Tack.

"I may be busy that night" he muttered straightening his tie.

"You busy, doing what?" Abbot said laughing.

"I don't know yet, got to look at my diary first, haven't I?" he said holding her stare.

"Anyway, I don't even know him" he added.

"I obviously don't know him either, but I might go, might be a fun night, calling him Charles all night." she said smiling.

They started to walk down the corridor and out into the car park.

"So, why are we going back to the scene of crime again, we won't find anything; it's already been thoroughly searched?"

He stood waiting at the car holding the door handle waiting for her to unlock it. She raised her arm, then pointed the remote pressing the 'open' button.

Finally, he opened his door, then slid into the passenger seat. Abbot climbed in, then turned the key in the ignition. They both wrapped their seatbelts around them.

They drove to the crime scene in silence. She done a number of twists and turns around the villages and towns until they reached the foot of Church Lane. Then came up against a "NO ENTRY' sign due to police incident.

Abbot parked her car at the top of the lane on a slight angle behind a panda car. She yanked on her handbrake, then they both unhooked their seatbelts. They both alighted the car and walked the rest of the way. The police cordon tape was still in place. A local uniformed police Constable was guarding the churchyard entrance. He recognised the two detectives then lifted up the police tape and waved them through.

"So, what are we looking for again?" inquired Peter's.

"I want to locate the murder weapon he was beaten to death with" she said putting her hands in her coat pockets.

"It's not going to be here; I've told you it's been searched from top to bottom."

"Right Sergeant, you look over there, I'll look over here" she said ignoring his question.

"SOCO and forensics have searched the whole churchyard, we're not going to find anything here."

"I know, but I want to search it myself" she said producing a pair of fingerless pink woolly gloves from her coat pocket.

Peter's looked at them and smiled to himself.

"What?"

"Nothing" he said walking off.

He could still hear Abbot from behind him saying "What?" again.

The wind blew coldly through the trees. Making the branches creek. Numerous single golden leaves blew past Abbot. Blowing her hair in all directions.

A couple of minutes later Peter's walked up to Abbot who was on all fours next to a big oak tree.

"Watch out, there's dog doings just there" he said blowing some warmth into his hands.

Abbot leapt on her feet.

"Ohh yuck, you could have told me?" She said brushing herself down.

"I just did."

"What do you want anyway Sergeant, you should be over there looking?" she said flipping her hair back behind her left ear.

"Have any of the rubbish bins been emptied since SOCO and forensics searched the place?" he asked curiously.

"How on earth would I know without looking, tell you what Sergeant, contact the local council and ask what day they should have been emptied and then you won't get too cold whilst you're standing there trying to look busy will you?" she said rolling her eyes at him.

"Hold on, I've got a better idea" he said looking down the path at the Constable in the distance.

"What's that then Sherlock?" she inquired sarcastically.

"I'll go and ask the Constable, he's been here all this time guarding the place, hasn't he?"

"Go on then, go and ask him" she said shaking her head at him.

He shortly returned with a grin on his face.

"Well, Sherlock?"

"Not as yet they did turn up, but he turned them away until a later date" he said looking smug at her.

"Right Sergeant, take that smug look off your face, you can look through every single bin and check them now can't you, I want no stone left unturned Sergeant?" she said smiling.

"Funny thing is it could be a stone we are looking for, the place is full of them, how will we know which ones?"

"If it's got blood on it dummy, now start looking, it's freezing standing here" she said clapping her fingers together.

After Peter's searched through endless rubbish bins and littering the path with empty bottles, and Coke cans. And the odd dead shriveled up bunch of flowers. He shouted over to Abbot.

"Over here, I may have found something."

Abbot raced over to where Peter's was standing. There lying in a pile of wind-swept leaves was a new six inch sharp bladed kitchen knife staring up at them.

Abbot crouched down to take a closer look. It had blood on the blade and on the handle.

"Ok Sergeant, bag it up and get it to forensics" she said excitedly.

"Eh have you got a bag, I left mine in my desk draw back at the station?" he said shrugging his shoulders.

"Oh, what you like, I've got loads in my glove compartment, in the car."

They both walked down the path together until they reached the gate. They turned right, and headed up the hill to Abbot's car. Peter's held the knife in between his thumb and forefinger. Carefully trying not to contaminate it.

As they reached Abbot's car. She leaned on the bonnet and lit a cigarette. Whilst Peter's looked in franticly through the glove compartment. After a couple of minutes rummaging and searching through the masses of empty crisp and sweet wrappers he slammed it shut in frustration.

"I can't find any."

Abbot looked back at him through the windscreen as she blew out a plume of smoke.

"You're not looking hard enough, they're in there somewhere!"

He scrambled out of the car with crisp and sweet wrappers around his feet. Some stuck to the bottom his shoes.

"You come and have a look then being it's your car?" He growled trying to rub the offending sweet wrappers onto the grass.

"I'm having a cigarette., I've worked hard looking for that on my knees all morning."

"Ohh and I haven't, OK, you can get your own bag from now on, I've had it with you, oh and you can put your own rubbish back in the glove compartment!" he said slamming the door shut.

He walked back down the hill to the uniformed Constable that was still guarding the churchyard gate.

After she'd finished her cigarette. She looked through her glovebox herself. She rolled her eyes at herself, as she couldn't find a forensic bag. She walked around to the rear of the car. She lifted her boot lid and found a plastic Tesco shopping bag. She pulled out the bag and placed the knife into it. She slammed down the boot lid.

She walked back down the hill towards Peter's and the Constable. She gave them both a reassuring smile as she approached them both.

"I'm sorry, I shouldn't have snapped, I've just got things on my mind at the minute" she said gently rubbing his arm.

"That's ok, don't worry, is there anything I can do?"

"Thank you, but not really."

They both started to walk slowly back to Abbot's car. Peter's slipped his hands into his pockets.

"Did you manage to find a bag?" he asked softly.

"Yeah."

"Oh good."

"Yeah, I couldn't find an evidence bag, so I used a supermarket carrier bag instead" she said winking.

"You can't use a supermarket carrier bag; it may contaminate the knife" he spluttered.

44

"I'll tell them when we get to forensics, it's the only one I could find, and tell them they don't issue enough out" she said opening her car door.

They both laughed as they climbed back into the car. She turned the key in the ignition to try and get warm. She turned halfway in her seat. Holding one hand on the steering wheel. The other on her lap.

"You know statistically nine times out of ten the killer knows the victim, in one way or another" she said leaning her head hard into the leather headrest.

"You think the tramp knew his killer?" he said distantly.

"Why, don't you think he did?" she asked frowning.

"I'm not too sure, it could have just been an opportunist killing" he said folding his arms and deep in thought.

"Yes true, but what possible motive would you have for killing someone who is down on their luck, you wouldn't, he's not going to have a wallet full of money, or be wearing valuable jewellery, would he, no, I think he knew his killer?"

"Do you think another tramp harboured a grudge and killed him perhaps?" he asked curiously.

"Quite possible, I suppose" she said sighing.

"I didn't even know we had vagrants on the island, they say that the Isle of Wight is the most popular destination on the south coast for tourists."

"Who said?"

"I read it in a tourist guidebook somewhere, oh some years ago now."

"They don't tell the tourists the crime rates, do they?" she said dryly.

"No, it would put them right off coming, wouldn't it?" he said looking out the window.

45

"I've got to say Sergeant, how come who ever searched that area didn't find the weapon, it was searched with a fine-tooth comb, how could they have missed it?"

"None of the officers would have overlooked it surely, unless it was put there after we'd searched the churchyard and the killer was hoping to use it again anytime soon" he added.

"A possibility" she thought.

Abbot carefully maneuvered around the parked-up panda car. She clipped the kerb as she turned hard right of her steering wheel. She glanced in her rear-view mirror as she changed up a gear. She pulled alongside the churchyards gate. She rolled down her window and beckoned the Constable over.

The Constable walked confidently over to her. He leaned down to her eye level.

"Constable has anyone entered this churchyard whilst you've been on duty?"

"No ma'am, but I've only been guarding this entrance, there's another round the back of the church, somebody could of came in it that way ma'am."

"What a fool I've been, Peter's, I didn't realise there was two entrances, thank you Constable" she said putting the car into gear.

She rolled up her window as she pulled away. Screeching the tyres as she did so.

"Remind me later Sergeant to visit the old lady, I want to know if she saw anybody prowling around in there. She might have seen something without realising it" she said engaging another gear.

A call came through the radio "Alfa victor, come in please," said the voice.

"Alfa victor" it sounds like a cough sweet."

They both laughed.

"Alfa victor here" he said straightening his face.

The radio crackled.

"Sergeant Hobbs and WPC Grange may have found a building with CCTV, do you want them to proceed ma'am?" asked the voice.

Static from the radio crackles the airwaves again.

"Where's their location, over?" The voice on the radio relayed back the location.

"Tell them to wait till myself and DS Abbot arrive, we're on our way now, over" he said replacing the radio in its holder just by the gear lever.

Chapter 7

An old man pulling a trolley full of shopping jumped in horror as Abbots tyres screeched to a sudden stop behind Sergeant Hobbs and WPC Granges panda car. The two detectives alighted from the car heading towards the bank. It was a large Victorian building with a weathered farecard and worn-down front steps. Above the main entrance hung a CCTV camera. Which pointed towards the top of the street.

"Let's hope we find something" she said sounding hopeful.

The two Constables who radioed in. Alighted their panda car. And approached the two detectives.

"Have you two been in yet?" asked Peter's rubbing his hands together.

"No Sergeant, we had instructions to wait until you arrived," said the WPC.

"Well done WPC, there's a cafe across the road, go and

have a cup of tea and we'll be over shortly." he said putting his hand in his pocket to produce some change.

"There you go, have one on me."

The two uniformed Constables thanked him as one took his money. They crossed the busy road once there was a gap in the flow of traffic. Then headed to the cafe leaving Abbot and Peter's standing just inside the bank's doorway.

As the two detectives walked in. They stood next to an old heater mounted onto a bright yellow wall. It wasn't giving out much heat.

"Can I help you at all?" asked the young clerk smiling.

Her smile quickly evaporated soon as they produced their warrant cards.

"We're investigating a murder that happened in the churchyard last night not too far away from here, we'd like to look through your CCTV if we may?" asked Abbot putting away her card.

"I'll have to ask my manager first" said the clerk walking off in the direction of the manager's office.

A couple of minutes later she came back. A queue had formed behind the two detectives. The couple behind was tutting and grumbling.

"This is the manager" the clerk said holding out her arm to introduce him.

He was a fair-haired man in his late fifties. Smartly dressed and businesslike.

"Hello, I'm Mr Edwards the manager of this branch, I'm told you want to look through our CCTV?" he said shaking their hands.

"If that's not a problem Sir?" said Peter's smiling rubbing his hands warm.

"No, no not a problem at all, I'll take you up to the CCTV room myself" he said directing them to follow him.

They went through a set of double doors down a long corridor and finally reached the CCTV room.

It was a small room with no windows. In there was a small desk and two plastic chairs. On a shelf above the table two monitors were placed. One camera was facing towards the front of the building. Whilst the other was facing towards the staff car park.

"You're telling me that this is your high-profile security system?" said Abbot irritated from the lack of equipment.

"The picture is so grainy, it's impossible to see anything" added Peter's.

He squinted at the fuzzy screens.

"What would you do if you had a robbery?" he asked gobsmacked.

"Well, what we do is that we keep taping over and over the same video tape, and I'm afraid that's why it's so grainy" he said coughing as his neck reddened.

"What's the point in having any CCTV at all if you keep taping over it?" Peter's exclaimed.

"It gives the customers a sense of security knowing we've got CCTV Sergeant" he said puffing out his chest pompously.

"Yeah, not a very good one at best, is it?" said Peter's tutting.

Abbot and Peter's sat down at the desk. Pushing their chairs in right against the desk. She pressed the PLAY button on the remote and started running the previous evenings tape. She scrolled back and forward on the video machine.

Two distort figures walked past the camera at the appointed time in question. But because the images were so grainy. It was hard to make out a formal identification. It could have been anyone.

They watched as the tape continued to play. They couldn't be sure it was their man. But it certainly looked like a possibility.

"What do you think?" asked Peter's tutting at the screen.

"Could well be Sergeant" she said watching the two figures disappear out of shot.

Abbot half-turned in her seat and looked back at the bank manager.

"I'm afraid we're going to have to take this video tape away for evidence, if that's alright Sir?"

"And what do you expect us to do if we have a robbery tonight with no video tape?" he asked indignantly.

"Well let's put it this way, it wouldn't make much of a difference really would it, especially with how poor quality your tapes are in, I wouldn't worry if I was you, Mr Edwards?"

Abbot rose to her feet then ejected the cassette tape and placed it into a dusty empty cassette box that was on the shelf. She held onto it as they all left the room.

The bank manager followed muttering grumpily under his breath about paying taxes.

A couple of minutes later, and the two detectives were walking over to the other side of the bustling street towards the cafe.

They noticed the two uniformed Constables sitting next to a warm inviting radiator at the farthest end of the cafe. They went and joined them. The walls were covered in various forms of sketching from around the island. One as far back as 1890.

It wasn't really busy in there. Considering how busy the street was. An elderly couple sat in the window watching people go by huddled up under their coats and scarves.

"Ehh a cup of tea and a currant bun please when you're

ready?" shouted Peter's in the direction of the waitress standing propping up the counter.

"Oh, I'll just get my own shall I Sergeant?" Abbot growled.

He shrugged his shoulders and smiled at her.

"We may have a positive identification Ma'am" said the WPC leaning towards Abbot as not to be heard.

"What do you mean?" asked Peter's whispering.

"Well when we came in and ordered our teas, I showed the chef over there the photo of the dead man, and he said it definitely looks like our man" she said quietly again.

Abbot looked around her. The chef was standing flirting next to the waitress. The odd laugh erupted from them both.

"I can't bear this any longer" said Abbot standing up from the table.

She walked over to them both. The chef who wore a greased stained pinafore looked like it hadn't been washed in a few years. The white towel that hung over his right shoulder didn't look too clever either.

The waitress skulked away pulling a face as Abbot approached the counter.

Abbot noticed the man's greasy looking grey hair. On which made her glad she hadn't ordered anything.

"Ehh, you told my WPC over there, that you may know the dead man that was murdered the other night?" she said standing away from the counter.

"Yes, that's the man, he and another tramp come in all the time, sit in the window they would, they could make a cup of tea last all day them pair, used to put my other customers off coming in."

"Looks like nothing's changed then, did you know his name or, where he used to sleep?" she said taking another step back.

"I know the other tramp called him Arthur, that's all I know" he said scratching his scalp.

The dandruff was dropping onto Peter's what looked like an out-of-date current bun.

"But I have no idea where he used to sleep" he added as an afterthought.

"Do you happen to know the other man's name at all?"

"I think, I heard him call him Albert" he said wrinkling his forehead in thought.

"Were there any fallouts with the two of them that you know of?"

"No, none at all, they were just two people down on their luck that's all, as I say they'd come in and sit in the window, watch the bank for a couple of hours and leave."

"Watch the bank, what do you mean?" she inquired wide-eyed.

"They'd just sit in that window, and watch the bank, well who came out of the bank more like."

"Anyone in particular?" she asked with a little hope.

"Mostly the bank manager, watched him like a hawk them two did."

She thought for a moment wondering why they would just watch the bank manager. Did they know him, or was there something more sinister in their watching him?

"Ok thank you for your time, you've been most helpful."

"That's quite alright my darling, here's your tea and there's his currant bun" he said winking.

She picked up the tray in disgust. Then went and sat back with the others.

Back in the freezing outer office. Abbot decided to hold a quick meeting.

"Ok listen up everyone, we think we may have found our man on CCTV today, it's very grainy but I want you

WPC Grange to go through that for me if you don't mind, he had a friend, our dead man, so we need to find him quick, I also want a team of four to search every piece of wasteland, bridge, or anywhere else they might try and keep warm" she said rubbing her hands together.

"What about hostels Ma'am?" suggested Sergeant Jones from the back of the room.

"Yes, ok hostels, anywhere else, oh, that reminds me, put my name down for your retirement party Charles" she shouted back at him.

"Ronnie Ma'am" he said correcting her.

"Sorry, Sergeant Jones" she said looking in his direction.

"Ronnie, my names Ronnie!"

"Yes, yes alright, ok, you found those hostels yet then Ronnie?" she said shaking her head.

"Not yet Ma'am, no."

"Well, come on get a move on, the quicker you move, the quicker you'll get to your retirement doo, oh, and by the way everybody, there's not enough budget for overtime this month so keep it near to office hours please, we don't want the Super from upstairs coming down on us like a ton of bricks like last month do we?"

The room filled with groans and muffled words. As the disgruntled officers got on with their work.

Chapter 8

The street was well lite and narrow with cars parked double-sided. She just about managed to find a space.

Engine still running to keep her warm. She watched the house interestingly for a few minutes. She lit a cigarette. Thick fog was starting to form around the car and in the street. The sodium streetlights were disappearing fast.

Then in the house. A dim lamp light shone from behind a draped curtain. She could just make out two dark figured silhouettes standing behind a door. A small child ran past the window laughing. Abbot knew it would be Jacob.

She opened her shoulder bag that was sitting next to her on the passenger's seat. She reached down and inside. Then produced her mobile phone. She scrolled through her personal contacts until she found the number she was looking for. Her thumb hovered over the familiar name and number. After a couple of long seconds. She pressed the familiar number. As the phone rang, she watched through Clare's window. After five rings. A familiar voice.

"Hello, it's me, I'll be late home tonight, can you get something out the freezer?" she said still looking through the window.

"Yeah, sure" said Richard on the other end of the line.

An awkward long silence from down the line. But now there was no sound in the background. It was now quiet.

"Do, you roughly know what time?" Richard finally said.

"I'm not sure, not too late I hope" she said pretending to laugh.

"Ok" Richard said ending the call.

She pressed the end call button her side. Putting the phone back into her bag. She put the car into gear then slowly drove off studying the black car that was parked next to Clare's red sports car.

Later that evening, Abbot sat around the kitchen table with files of case notes on one side of her. And a bottle of white wine on the other. She was so desperate to catch the other tramp. She felt guilty about snapping at Sergeant Jones earlier. It wasn't his fault. He's just doing his job. But the pressure was mounting up.

She re-examined the case file notes and photos of the man's injuries in between long gulps of wine.

After a few hours of drinking and sifting through the case files. She glanced down at her wristwatch, it read nine thirty five pm. She reached over and picked up the phone that lay next to her under a mountain of paperwork. She scrolled through the contacts list until she came to the number she was looking for. She hesitated for a long second. Then pressed it. After three rings, another familiar voice.

"Hey, I haven't disturbed you, have I?" she asked putting her hand up to her forehead.

"No, no, what is it?"

"Do, you want to join me with a glass of fine white, or we could catch up on some paperwork?"

"What about Richard?"

"He's not in, and the girls are having a sleepover at my mother's tonight" she said picking up her half empty glass.

"I'll just get ready."

"Right, I shall see you soon" she said smiling pressing the end call button.

She placed the empty glass down onto the table. She rose to her feet feeling lightheaded. She rushed through the kitchen to the foot of the stairs. She climbed the stairs, then turned right into the bathroom. She switched on the shower button, and then took a quick shower. After she dried off, she went into her bedroom to find some comfortable clothes. She found a woolly low-cut jumper. And a pair of tight blue jeans. Shortly after she'd brushed her hair, a light knock at the front door. She rushed out of the bedroom and down the stairs. She stopped and glanced in the hallway mirror to glance at herself. She shuffled her jumper a little down over her shoulders exposing her bra strap slightly. She turned slightly, then opened the door. Then let Peter's in.

"Ahh good your just in time to pour me another drink Sergeant" she said shutting the door behind him.

He stepped over the threshold, from out of the nighttime chill. He looked at Abbot's beauty as shuffled out of his coat in the hallway. Abbot smiled as she took his coat off him then hung it over the bannister rail.

"Let's go and sit in the living room, it's cosier in there" she said heading in there first.

"How many you had, looks like you've had a few already?" he inquired following her into the room.

He wondered over to the window, then sat down on the sofa.

"Not, as many as I would like" she said pouring another glass.

"I can't stay too long, as my landlady bolts the door at eleven."

With two drinks in her hands, she passed the other glass of wine to Peter's with a reassuring smile. He reached out his hand, then took it off her. She flopped down next to him. Putting her arm up against her head.

"Don't you have a key then?" she said taking a sip of wine.

"Yeah, but she gets funny if you get in late, it sets the dog off barking and it wakes the whole house."

"Tell her you're a copper, and she might let you stay out a wee bit longer" she said from behind her glass.

"I think its best I leave, you've obviously had too much to go through any kind of paperwork or have a proper conversation with."

"Please, don't go Sergeant, stay a while and enjoy one with me" she said licking her lips.

"Oh, alright just the one, I'm not very good with drink" he said leaning back into the sofa cushions.

She gulped her drink back in one go, then rose to her feet and poured herself another glass. She went back over to the sofa sitting back down. Putting one leg up on the sofa. The other under her bottom.

"Meaning what exactly?" she asked leaning back sideways against the cushions.

"Well, I get tipsy after just the one" he said with a chuckle.

"Well, we'll have to see to that as you don't get drunk then Sergeant, won't we?"

"So, have you ever been married Sergeant?" she asked curiously lightly circling the top of the glass with her index finger.

"I nearly was, but it went wrong, we got engaged, but she got cold feet and told me she didn't want to get married, she said she wanted more out of life first before she committed" he chuckled dryly.

"How long ago was that because, you've never told me, and I've been working with you on and off for years?"

"About two years ago now, or near to it, I can't remember now" he said shrugging his shoulders.

"Have you seen her around since you parted?" she asked taking a sip of wine.

"No, she moved back in with her parents in Warwickshire, then we lost touch."

"You'll find someone, someday, your handsome enough, you've got to be a wee bit more confident and then you'll be fine, then you could pick and choose anyone" she suggested feeling a little more tipsy.

"Oh, I don't know, maybe I'm not cut out to be with anyone" he said gloomily.

"What about that WPC on the front desk, she seems nice?"

"I'm not really looking for anyone at the moment, I just want to concentrate on my transfer to the mainland. I'm proud of where I've got to in my life, it means a lot to me to be a good detective."

"And you are a good detective, you work hard, and you get the job done, that's the sign of a good copper" she said nodding in agreement.

The room felt warm and relaxing, in the dim lamp glow. It gave the room some kind of ambiance and atmosphere for them both.

A coal fire snapped and crackled. Abbots deep brown eyes glistened and sparkled in the fire light, as another ember died.

Time just stood still for a couple of seconds. Neither spoke to each other, but only looked deep into each other's eyes. Peter's leaned forward, and reached for a glass from her hand. He placed the glass onto the coffee table infront of him, then turned back towards her. She looked beautiful with her hair resting on her bare shoulders. His eyes was now feeling full of pleasure and desire. He reached over for her hand. She reached out to hold it. He gently stroked the back of it.

He could smell her expensive lingering perfume. Then with his other hand. He started to stoke her neck. Then her ears. Her smooth skin felt soft and warm. He slowly lurched forward. Kissing her soft inviting lips passionately.

"If you want me to stop, then tell me now!"

"Just shut up and kiss me."

With adrenaline and one and a half bottles of wine pumping around inside her. She felt like she wanted to be a naughty teenager again. She reached forward throwing herself into his strong arms. Their wine drenched lips locked tightly together.

They both rose to their feet, then sat in the heat of the fire. Now the alcohol was taking over.

Their lips met again, for a long second. She leaned into him, then started to unbutton his shirt. He watched her undo them slowly, one by one. As she got nearer to the bottom button, he clenched her hand, forcing her to stop.

"What's the matter?" she asked frowning.

"I just don't think it's the right thing to do" he said shamefully.

"But I thought you fancied me?"

"I do, but..." he said cutting himself off.

60

"But what?" she asked feeling rejected.

"Its awkward."

"Why?"

"Because we both work together, so let's keep it professional" he said softly.

"Ok, yes, sorry your right, I don't know what came over me."

"It's ok, I understand" he said rising to his feet.

The next thing she was awoken from the sound of the front door closing. She must have fallen asleep on the sofa from the amount of alcohol.

At first, she thought it was Peter's leaving. But he'd left hours ago. She'd fallen asleep on the sofa.

On slowly getting up. She turned on the light yawning. She checked her wristwatch. It read two thirty am.

She carefully opened the living room door. Then crept across the hallway and into the kitchen. It was Richard. He was sitting at the kitchen table holding his head up with his hands.

"You're late, what time do you call this?" she growled with irritation.

"Yes sorry, the meeting went on longer than expected, and then a few of us went onto the pub. I didn't mean to wake you."

"Glad you did, I was flat out on the sofa" she said sighing.

She absentmindedly walked around him and took two cups out from the cupboard. And filled the kettle with water.

"What was the meeting about?"

"Oh, nothing much really, I wasn't paying much attention it was boring really" he said stretching out his arms in front of him on the table.

"Oh right, ok I'm going to bed" she said yawning again.

"Ehh Karen, just before you go, there's something I need to tell you" he said hesitantly.

"Oh yeah, can't it wait till tomorrow, I'm shattered" she said tensing up.

She thought she knew what was coming. She'd witnessed it earlier with her own eyes. She turned back towards him.

"What is it, you want to tell me?"

He became ridged and uncomfortable in his chair. He stood up grating the chair along the tiled floor.

"Well, nothing really, it's just that I want to tell you now in case you're working late again tomorrow night."

"Ok Richard, what is it, you've got to tell me, you can't just leave me in suspense?" she said holding his gaze.

"I've been asked at the office by means of a promotion, if I'd like to run their Liverpool office, and I've accepted."

"What?" she spat out.

He shrugged his shoulders nervously.

"And you've accepted, and you didn't even think to discuss the matter with me first?" she said aggressively.

"But I thought we was going to have a break from each other, that's why I excepted it?"

"Oh, and what happens now then, we can't just up and leave, I've got my job to consider, I'm in the middle of a murder investigation, what about the girls schooling, where we live, have you considered any of these issues Richard, or are you just thinking about yourself again?"

"I had to make a quick decision, I couldn't refuse the opportunity, so I accepted it on the spot, but I'm going on my own" he said refusing to look at her anymore.

"So, how quick will this change of office be?" she asked staring at the floor.

"By the end of next week" he said quietly.

He distanced himself from his angry wife. He picked up the two cups and placed them back into the cupboard.

"By the end of next week, have you gone raving mad, and why have they asked you to go, and no one else?"

"Because I'm good at my job, that's why" he shouted.

"And so am I Richard, and so am I" she said turning to walk out the door.

"But I've just said I'm going on my own I didn't even want to move down here in the first place, I was quite happy in Glasgow, but I made that decision, with you, and Sophie, I've had my time here and I think it's time I moved on within the company."

"Just with the company?" she asked glaring over at him.

"What do you mean?" he said awkwardly.

She moved further into the kitchen. And folded her arms as she leaned up against the door frame.

"I saw your car parked outside Clare's house tonight, was that a quick decision too, you wasn't in a meeting at all tonight were you, you were in her house doing heaven knows what, but the thing is I rang you tonight, to say I was going to be late, I was ringing you from outside her house."

"What?" he spat the word out.

"How longs it been going on for Richard, answer me that?"

He looked uncomfortable with himself. He didn't say a word. Not even after a long awkward silence.

"Fine, I'll be sleeping on the couch tonight, do what you want Richard, I don't care anymore?"

Richard could see the disappointment on her face. She turned away from him in disgust. Then walked away into the lounge slamming the door hard behind her.

Chapter 9

The following morning Abbot and Peter's drove in silence to the old lady's house who discovered the body in the graveyard. They drove down a yellow leafy narrow lane that was barely wide enough to fit a car. Bare undergrowth and branches scrapped alongside of Abbots car noisily. She indicated right. Then turned off the muddy lane and into the occupier's drive.

The cars tyres scrunched on the gravel. The two detectives unhooked their seatbelts. The women of the house stood at her front door, as Abbot alighted her car. Peter's slammed his door shut behind him. Peter's smiled at the women as he approached her. Whilst Abbot wrapped herself tighter into her coat.

The whole of the house with its black granite brickwork had weathered from standing proud for centuries. Over the front door hung patches of ivy that had been clipped neatly here and there in between the high Malian Windows. On the far side of the house stood a high angled chimney. On which black smoke bellowed.

"Hello Mrs Dawkins, do you remember me, I spoke to you on the night you found the body in the graveyard?" said Peter's introducing himself.

"Oh yes I remember, such a nice man you are" she said holding the door.

"This is my superior, DS Karen Abbot" he said smiling.

A man's faint voice shouted from a distance away. As well as the dog barking.

"Don't keep them standing at the door like you do them Jehovah Witnesses."

"We just wondered if we could have a chat with you, see if you can remember anything about the other night madam?" he said raising his voice over the sound of the barking dog.

"Like what dear?" she asked frowning.

"May we come inside Mrs Dawkins?" suggested Peter's.

"I tell you what Mrs Dawkins you, make a nice cup of tea and we'll wipe our feet on the way in, how does that sound?" suggested Abbot blowing into her hands.

The women opened the door wider for them both to enter. Both detectives wiped their feet on the mat inside the hallway.

The woman shuffled past them both to reach the kitchen. Abbot and Peter's made their way into the living room, over the way from the kitchen.

Abbot sat next to the coal fire that crackled and snapped in the grate. From which the heat was rising from the flames. Peter's sat on the edge of the same sofa as Abbot did. Peter's looked over at the husband wrapped under a blanket. Soon the women entered the room with a tray full of tea and biscuits.

The woman placed the tray on a coffee table near to the fire. The woman sat down opposite them both fluffing up her pillows. The husband let out a loud snort as Peter's reached inside his jacket pocket for his notebook.

"Now Mrs Dawkins, can you remember anything you might have forgot to tell me in your original statement, from last night?" asked Peter's quietly opening his notebook.

"I don't think so dear, I told you I was walking up past the church when I saw what I thought was a Guy."

"What made you think it was a Guy?" asked Peter's frowning.

"Well, I just presumed because it was Bonfire night."

"That's ok Mrs Dawkins, its an easy mistake to make."

"The thing is, I had a funny feeling I was being followed, but that was before I got to the churchyard though, I stopped and turned around to see if anyone was there but there wasn't, I remember a young boy asking me to give him a penny for his Guy, but I rushed past him."

"Can you describe the boy, Mrs Dawkins?" asked Abbot carefully.

"I didn't get a look at him I'm afraid, as I said I just rushed past him" she said reaching for her tea.

"You say you might have heard someone following you."

"Yes."

"How can you be certain?"

"It sounded like footsteps behind me" she said taking a sip of tea.

"Do you think it could have been the young boy?" suggested Peter's.

"No, I put it down that I was being followed, I've never been so scared in all my life; I've walked that path for years" she said sniffling.

"I understand that Mrs Dawkins" said Peter's with sympathy in his voice.

"So did you happen to see anyone in the churchyard before, or after you discovered the body?" asked Abbot impatiently again.

"No, there's not much light by the church, the vicar ought to put some proper lighting, it's not safe" she said in reaching for a digestive biscuit.

"I'll have a word with the vicar" said Abbot sarcastically.

"Oh thank you dear" said the woman sounding pleased.

"Ok Mrs Dawkins, thank you for your time and your lovely cup of tea, sorry we haven't got time to drink it" said Abbot placing her cup back on the tray.

She kicked Peter's discreetly in the shin as a sign to hurry him up from his tea and interview. Both detectives got up and headed for the front door. The woman headed in front of them to open the door. Abbot and Peter's gave the woman a smile as they stepped out into the cold November air.

When they were walking back towards the car. Peter's asked Abbot what her problem was?

"What do you mean Sergeant, I don't have a problem?" she growled.

"You, in there, making me rush my tea, nearly spilling it down my tie" he said angrily.

"She obviously didn't see anyone or anything, or else she would have told us" she said opening her car door.

Abbot looked at him in frustration from over the car roof. She stood for a long second before she climbed into the car.

"Plus, she was starting to get right on my last nerve" she said opening the car door.

"Go on, admit it, you're feeling guilty and regret about last night, aren't you?"

She turned the key in the ignition and wrapped her seatbelt around her. Peter's did the same, as he waved to the woman still standing at the door. She engaged the car into gear, then drove back down the narrow muddy lane. Once she'd reached the end of the lane, before she turned right onto the main road she sighed deep into the air.

"It's got nothing at all to do with last night if you must know" she said changing up a gear.

"Well, what then?" he asked folding his arms.

"I've got things on my mind at the minute, that's all, I can't think straight" she said checking her rearview mirror.

"Ok like what?"

"You wouldn't understand."

"Why wouldn't I understand?"

"Because it's family business, that's why" she said changing the car into a different gear.

"And what makes you think I wouldn't understand family business?"

"Because mines getting complicated that's why."

"In what way is it getting complicated?" he asked frowning.

"I think you know why?"

"No, I don't."

"You and me last night, that shouldn't of happened, we have to keep our work separate from our private lives."

"But you were willing to comply."

"I know, and now I regret it."

"Do you?"

She didn't bother answering the question, as she indicated right into the police stations car park. She yanked on her handbrake, then alighted the car leaving Peter's behind. She walked through the set of double doors at the main entrance and into the lobby area. WPC Grange was tending to a man on the front desk. Abbot just leaned rudely over the man's shoulder.

"Any messages for me WPC?"

"Yes, Ma'am a couple of Constables managed to track down the other tramp" she said excusing the man for a second.

"Where did they find him?"

"Sitting in the cafes window Ma'am, the owner rang in."

"Oh, wonderful where is he now?" asked Abbot trying to punch her security number into the security door.

"In the interview room."

"WPC, what is the flaming number to this door?" she said frustrated gritting her teeth.

The WPC gave her a smile as she pressed her buzzer from under the desk. Then let her in manually.

"Didn't you get the email Ma'am?"

"What email, I never received one?" she said holding open the door.

"The whole of the station had one."

"Did we WPC?"

"We had to change the security number because someone left the security door open and helped themselves and stole all the toilet rolls from the ladies' toilets!"

"How does someone leave a police station, with a load of stolen toilet rolls without being seen?" she said rolling her eyes.

"Well, we did catch the perpetrator."

"And?"

"And their going to get community service Ma'am."

"Don't tell me there's a shortage of loo rolls?" suggested Abbot rolling her eyes again.

"Not anymore Ma'am, we've hidden them in the cleaning cupboard now."

"The perpetrator took them out in bin liners, we didn't know until we ran out of them" said the WPC.

"How careless."

"I know."

"And next time could you make sure nobody gets past this door again without the proper authorization."

"Ma'am."

Peter's kept in silence as he stood back listening to the conversation. He gave the WPC a reassuring smile as he followed Abbot through the security door.

She slammed the door behind her. Abbot had about more than she could take. She walked irritated down the corridor. As she approached the interview room. She smelt something. Something she couldn't put her finger on.

"What's that awful smell?" she said sniffing the air.

"Could be the canteen food?"

"No, that smells worse than this, don't tell me, it's the canteens sinks blocked again, it was unbearable last time?" she said pulling a face.

They finally reached the interview room. As Abbot opened the interview room door. The aroma could only be described as rotting vegetables.

She entered the room, and crunched up her face.

"Can someone open a window in here, I can't take it any longer?" she said complaining screwing up her nose.

"We can't."

"Why?" she screeched.

"There isn't one in here" he said sheepishly as he moved out of range from the aroma.

Her temper wasn't something to be trifled with.

"Blooming marvelous, we could hold the interview out in the car park, at least I'd be able to breathe out there" she said shaking her head.

She managed to rein in her anger. By taking in a sharp intake of air. She pulled out a chair from underneath the table.

Then sat down opposite a middle-aged man with a cigarette-stained beard. He was wearing a green woolly hat. A dirty over coat and a pair of black fingerless gloves.

"Am I going to be arrested?" asked the man leaning forward in his chair.

"No, this is only an informal interview, so I'm not going to record it, instead my Sergeant here, is going to write it down as a statement, ok?" she said sitting away from the table folding her arms.

"Am I going to be arrested?" asked the tramp again.

"You should be, just for carrying that smell around with you, all day" she said screwing up her nose again in disgust.

"Did you happen to kill a man two nights back, answering to the name of Albert?" she said bluntly.

"Good god no, I might be down on my luck lady, but I wouldn't harm or kill my only friend" he said genuinely.

"Ah, ok then, a friend you say?"

"Yeah, the only one I've had in years, you got a cigarette darling?"

"Sorry, I left my cigarettes in my car, and I'm not your darling" she said patronizingly.

She looked over at Peter's who stood by the door.

"Sergeant, have you got a cigarette for this man?" she said looking back at the tramp.

"But I don't smoke" he said patting his pockets.

"We'll go and ask someone who does Sergeant, this man has rights too you know?"

He left the room abruptly slamming the door behind him. He returned a few minutes later wherein he handed the tramp a cigarette.

71

"Thank you, got a light?" said the tramp putting the cigarette up to his mouth.

"Well Sergeant?" she said looking frustrated at Peter's again.

"No, I didn't get a light" he said shaking his head and left the room for a second time.

As he entered the room. He gave the tramp a box of matches. Then he noisily sat down next to Abbot. Throwing her a dirty look.

"Anything else before we go on any further?" she asked through a thick cloud of smoke blowing in her face.

"A cup of tea wouldn't go a miss, with two sugars?" said the man looking at Peter's.

Peter's stood up for a third time. But resisted the urge to strangle the man. Just as he was about to leave the room Abbot glared at Peter's.

"Oh Sergeant, on the way back, see if you can find a can of air freshener or something, and bring it in with you, if you wouldn't mind?"

He left the room. Slamming the door hard behind him in frustration. She checked her wristwatch.

"How long does it take the fool?" she thought.

Eventually, they were ready to conduct the interview. With tea on the table. A cigarette in the man's hand. And a healthy dose of sprayed air freshener that permeated nicely around the room.

"So, you didn't kill your friend Albert, but do you know who may have done?" she suggested carefully.

The man slurped loudly on his tea. Whilst this question was asked.

"No" he said taking a long drag on his cigarette.

"All I know is, he said he was onto something big" he added exhaling a cloud of smoke.

"Something big?" Peter's repeated frowning.

"Yeah, said he'd met an old pal, and said it was going to make him rich" he said taking another drag on his cigarette.

He leaned forward and picked up his tea from off the table.

"He said that would show them" he said still slurping.

"Show who?" inquired Abbot.

"He didn't say, just kept saying that would show them."

"Who was this pal he'd met, do you know?" she asked thoughtfully.

"No, he didn't tell me his name, he just kept referring to him as his pal" he said scratching his head.

"Did you plan to meet up together, two nights ago, say about nine pm?" asked Peter's.

"No, he said he'd got to meet his new pal."

"Do you know where he was going to meet this new pal of his?" she asked hopeful.

"He told me, in the graveyard, he said where it would be 'DEAD QUIET'."

"Yeah, 'DEAD QUIET' being the operative word in a graveyard" she said rolling her eyes at Peter's.

"And at what time did he say he was going to meet this new pal of his?"

"He told me he was meeting him around nine thirty, or ten o'clock, something like that, I can't remember" he said coughing into his fist.

"Well at ten o'clock, a witness phoned the station to say they'd found a body in the graveyard, so where were you in this time frame?" inquired Peter's frowning.

"Out walking."

"Out walking where, it was Bonfire night two nights ago?" added Peter's.

"Just walking, I can't remember" the tramp said shrugging his shoulders."

"So, whoever killed your friend, killed him moments before he was found, so do you know anything about that?" she said softly.

"I don't know anything, I wasn't there, was I?"

"So, all we've got off you, is that you were out walking somewhere, it's not a very solid alibi, is it all you've told us is you went for a walk but can't remember where, it's not looking good for you at the moment is it?" added Peter's placing his pen down on the table.

"No" said the man beginning to look troubled.

"No, so where were you walking?" asked Peter's again slowly.

The man paused for a minute to drink the last few dregs of his tea. A couple of long seconds after he replaced the empty cup onto the table in front of him.

"Alright, I was there, I followed him at a safe distance so that he wouldn't see me."

"Then what?" inquired Abbot frowning.

"I wanted to know who he was meeting, he got to the graveyard, then stood at the gate for a few minutes, then he walked further in and went past the church."

"Go on." Abbot said enthusiastically.

"Well, just as he past the church, there was this figure, I couldn't see who it was, they started arguing the pair of them and then the next thing I saw him hit Albert over the head with something heavy" he said getting upset.

"So, you must of been close to see him hit over the head with something heavy?" said Abbot dryly.

"I waited in the bushes, out of sight of the moonlight, anyway, I couldn't see what it was as it was too dark" he said bowing his head.

"So, what happened next?" asked Abbot curiously.

"Then the figure ran off into the darkness when he saw an old lady walking her dog, I'd recognized her earlier because she was in front of me when I was following Albert."

"The old lady said she felt she was being followed" said Peter's turning to Abbot.

"Can you describe this figure, was it a man or a woman, would you know?" she asked sounding hopeful.

"I couldn't see properly it was far too dark, and the figure wore all black clothes, but it looked definitely like a man."

"Oh."

"Yeah, you could tell by the way the figure ran off."

"Was the figure tall or average height, can you remember?" asked Abbot frowning.

"No, I told you, it was too far away from me, and it was too dark to see anything."

"But you just said, you saw the figure hit your friend over the head with something heavy, if it was that dark how do you know it was heavy?"

"Can you give us a description of any kind?" asked Peter's scribbling down the man's every words.

"No, only he was wearing black clothes, that's all I remember."

"So, it was definitely a man then?"

"When did I say it was a man?"

"You did just a second ago" said Peter's pointing his pen at him.

"No, I said a figure!" said the tramp irritated.

"That's a big help that is, it could be the whole of the Isle of Wight for all we blooming know."

"Am I going to be arrested now officer?"

"No, not today, but why I don't know." suggested Peter's placing his pen down on the desk.

Abbot sighed deeply into the air as she looked over her right shoulder at Peter's.

"Sergeant could you take this man down to the cells, get him a shower and see if we've got any clean clothes in the lost property cupboard?"

"Ok" he said grating his chair from under the table.

"Oh, and when you've done that, can you make sure he gets a decent meal from the canteen?" she said softly.

"You sure that's wise?"

"Meaning?" asked Abbot frowning.

"Meaning you know what the food's like in the canteen, what if he gets food poisoning?"

"Just don't offer him any meat pies, I've seen how they make them down that canteen!" she said crunching up her face.

"Umm ok" he said slipping one hand into his trouser pocket.

Then Peter's smiled at the man and indicated him to follow him. Abbot flipped her hair behind her left ear and stood up. She half turned as the both of them were about to leave the room.

"Ohh and when you've finally done them tasks, can you spray this room with the rest of that air freshener?"

"Why?" Peter's asked frowning.

"Because it smells like an allotment patch in here" she said quietly.

Chapter 10

Later that night. Chief Constable Green walked past Abbot's office and noticed the dim lamp glow coming from underneath her door. He knocked lightly then popped his head around the door.

"Ah you still here Abbot, everyone else has gone home?" he said walking over to her desk.

"Yes Sir, I just need to catch up on some paperwork" she said sighing.

"So, how's the church murder coming along?" he inquired resting on the edge of her desk.

"That's the report I'm trying to catch up on Sir."

An awkward smile glanced past them both. Abbot held his stare, she leaned back into her high-backed chair, whilst folding her arms.

"Any nearer to catching anyone yet?" he asked curiously.

"Not yet Sir, but we found the knife that was used."

"Well, that's a start I suppose, any fingerprints on it?" he asked yawning from the back of his hand.

"No, not yet I'm waiting on forensics to get back to me Sir, but we still haven't found the weapon that killed him as yet."

"You should go home Abbot, it's getting late."

"I know Sir."

"What do you mean by that Abbot?"

"Oh nothing" she said unfolding her arms.

"It must mean something, you're the only one here, and it's nearly ten o'clock, that's not like you at all Abbot."

He moved from off the edge of the table then sat opposite her.

"How's Richard and the girls?"

"Oh, they're fine, thank you Sir."

"Just fine.

"Oh, you know me Sir."

"So, what's on your mind?" he asked frowning whilst folding his arms.

"Nothing Sir, I just want to get my paperwork done without any distractions at home that's all."

"Oh, come off it Abbot, I know you better than that, you've been at this station for a number of years now, I think I should know when one of my finest detectives has something pressing on their mind."

She flipped her hair back behind her left ear, she said looking down at the floor uncomfortably.

"I think Richards having an affair."

"And what makes you think that?" he asked frowning.

"Because I went to the house where the woman lives, and saw his car parked outside."

"Was it definitely Richard's car, you saw?" he asked softly.

"Yeah, it had his private number plate on it, I knew it was his because I bought it him for his forty second birthday present, plus Grace saw him kissing this woman in the school playground."

"So have you spoken to him about it?"

"Yeah, when he came home in the early hours this morning."

"And what did he say?"

"He claimed he was in a meeting all day, and it ran over time, then him and a few mates went to the pub."

"So, what did he say to that?"

"Nothing really, he didn't even deny it, he said that his office has asked him to run their Liverpool branch because he's so good at his job."

"And what's wrong with that?" he asked frowning.

"He said he wants me and the girls to go with him."

"Oh, I see, well surely, he can't be seeing anyone if he wants you and the girls to go with him and move all the way to Liverpool?" he said crossing his legs.

"Well, there's the problem."

"What is?"

"Well, I phoned his office and asked about the move to Liverpool."

"And?"

"And they haven't even got an office in Liverpool, their nearest office is in Birmingham."

"Oh, I see now, things don't look good, do they?"

"No."

"I should see how things develop, and if things are no different in a few days suggest…" he said cutting himself off shrugging his shoulders.

"The thing is every time we talk it always ends in an argument, I've even suggested we separate for a wee while, see how things go."

"Ok, but I've got to ask you this Abbot, do you think

this will cloud your judgement on the case?"

"What do you mean?" she asked now

frowning leaning forward in her chair.

"Well, what I mean is, if you need time off to get things sorted with Richard, I understand, you know what I'm trying to say Abbot?" he said with a reassuring smile.

"Thank you, Sir, but I'll be fine, us Scott's are made from girders, as the iron brew advert once said."

They both laughed, then Green rose to his feet, and then headed for the door. He pulled down on the door handle. Then opened it slightly. He turned on his heels, then looked back in Abbot's direction.

"Turn off the lights when you leave won't you Abbot?" he said softly.

"Thank you, I will Sir."

She watched him as he disappeared behind the door. Shutting it quietly behind him.

Chapter 11

The following morning Abbot was in her office bright and early. But outside it was still dark.

"Blimey, did you wet the bed this morning or something then?" suggested Peter's laughing propping up against her office door frame.

"No, I did not, and stop being so vulgar."

"So, you're going tonight then?"

"Going where, and why do you have to be so blooming chirpy at this time in the morning, it's not even eight o'clock yet?" she said checking her wristwatch.

"To Ronnie Jones's retirement doo" he said winking at her from the other side of the room.

"You got to be kidding me, I'd completely forgot about that, is that tonight?"

"Yes, so you didn't manage to find a babysitter then?"

"Does it sound like it Sergeant; I'd completely forgotten about asking anyone?"

She said folding his gaze from across the room.

"Typical" he said rolling his eyes at her.

"I tell ya what Sergeant you could do it; you're not going are you, you've got no one to go with anyway, have you?" she said sarcastically.

"Oh yes I have, and I am" he said smiling from ear to ear.

"Sergeant, instead of leaning up against my door frame and letting in all the cold, go and get some work done, you're driving me insane" she said rolling her eyes at him in frustration.

He rolled his eyes back at her, as he slowly walked away. He chuckled to himself as he approached his desk. He leaned down then switched on his computer and waited for it to show some kind of life. From time to time, he kept looking through the corner of his eyes at Abbots beauty through her office window.

Abbot picked up her mobile telephone from off her desk and rested it against her ear. Then punched in the number to the forensic lab. After a few rings, the Doctors familiar voice echoed down the line.

"Ah doc, glad I've caught you, any news on the knife yet?"

"Yes, we've found a partial fingerprint."

"Oh brilliant" she said sounding excited.

"Ahh don't get too excited Abbot, the fingerprint is not on any database so we couldn't find a match unfortunately" he said killing her excitement.

"Oh, poo pants, so he hasn't got a criminal record then?"

"Doesn't look like it at the moment."

"Can we get any DNA then doc?"

"We would need something to compare it with first" he said gloomily.

"Oh, ok it was just a thought anyway doc."

She paused for a long second before she was about to replace the receiver. But she thought of something else.

"Oh, before you go doc, were there any other foreign fibres on the body?"

"No, we've searched, not even anything under the fingernails."

"Oh right, I was just going to ask about his fingernails doc, thanks you" she said ending the call. Sergeant Peter's wondered back over to her office as he just got off his own desk phone.

"Don't you dare prop that door frame up again Sergeant" she growled putting her mobile back onto her desk.

"No, it's worse than that, there's another body been discovered in the graveyard."

"What?" she shouted.

"There's another body discovered in the…?"

"I heard you the first time Sergeant." interrupting him.

Now the crimes had just become even more complicated. If that wasn't enough.

The rain pelted hard against her windscreen. Her wash wipers slapped in time to the speed of the rain. She done a number of twists and turns down through the back streets and the lanes. She splashed in the puddles making waves from her tyres. She pulled up alongside a patrol car that was parked on a slight angle, and where she'd been parked hours earlier. She yanked on her handbrake, as she unhooked her seatbelt. She pulled her key out the ignition. Then she opened her umbrella as she alighted the car.

Peter's alighted the car and huddled into his jacket. They both walked up the churchyards soaking wet pavement to where a tent had now been erected. The tent was erected over the body to try and preserve some kind of evidence. But in this dreadful weather most of it would have been washed away with the rain. So, with possibly no forensics on the body. It wasn't going to be easy.

Peter's tried his hardest to get under Abbot's umbrella for shelter. But it was proving harder than he thought.

As they both approached the tent. Flashes of light from the SOCO team lit up the confined space for a brief second as they were taking photographs from every angle possible. Abbot stopped for a long second, to shake the rain off her umbrella before she entered. Pulling the zip to one side. Both detectives went inside.

The soaking wet body lay face down with his arms stretched out before him. It also had the hallmarks of the last victim. A severe blow to the back of the head. Just then the Doctor was about to turn the body over onto its back. It was clear to see a single stab wound to the upper chest area. Only this time. The victim wasn't a tramp.

"Morning doc, how long would you say he's been dead?" inquired Abbot crouching down next to the Doctor whilst he was examining the body.

"Oh, I'd say at least nine hours, I'll know better when I get him back to the lab."

"You said that last time doc" she said raising herself up.

"I know but it was pitch black then" he said still crouching over the body.

"He's soaking wet, and riggers set in so, he's definitely been here all night I'm afraid Abbot" he suggested, raising himself up too.

"It looks like the same M.O. to me doc, looks like he's been also hit over the head with a heavy object, then stabbed" she said looking down at the body.

"Yes exactly" the Doctor muttered.

"Umm."

"But at least I found this in his inside coat pocket Abbot" he said handing her over a small red notebook.

"Thanks doc" she said frowning at the object.

"I'll start on him soon as I get back to the lab."

"Thanks again doc" she said quickly flicking through the notebook.

"Think nothing of it Abbot."

After quickly flicking through the notebook, she slipped it into her coat pocket to inspect later.

"I tell you what doc, if you didn't have lunch today you could get the postmortem done quicker?" she suggested smiling.

"It's not a five-minute job you know Abbot" he said shaking his head at her in frustration.

"Yes, yes ok doc, I understand but just keep me informed" she said rolling her eyes.

The two detectives exited the tent then walked down the still wet footpath back towards the local Constable who was sheltering in his panda car. He immediately wound his window down as he saw them approaching. The rain had now eased. But still damp in the air.

"Morning Ma'am."

"So, who found the body then Constable?" she asked leaning down to his eye level.

"A workman Ma'am, he's sitting over there in his vehicle, keeping dry" he said pointing to a white transit van that was parked up in the car park area.

"Yes, ok then Constable, you sit there and stay dry in your nice warm car, whilst we get wet, and do all the leg work in the rain."

The uniformed Constable stretched out his arm for his door handle.

"No, don't worry yourself Constable, I have my nice

big umbrella, it saves me from getting wet" she said sarcastically.

Peter's chuckled to himself as they both walked off. Leaving the Constable red faced and embraced. They walked back past the erected tent. Finally reaching the workman sitting in his van. Abbot tapped on his window with her folded up index finger. The workman rolled down his window. He looked pale faced and in shock.

"Hello, my name is DS Karen Abbot, and this is Sergeant Peter's, I've been informed that you found the body. Is that correct?"

"Yes, just over there by that big oak tree" he said shivering.

By the sour smell on his breath, he'd not long been sick. Abbot moved back slightly crunching up her face whilst trying to hold his stare. Peter's slipped his cold hands into his trouser pockets.

"So, what can you tell me?" asked Abbot, still holding his stare.

"I was digging a hole for a funeral tomorrow morning. I usually have someone with me, but he called in sick this morning.

"Lucky for him then" she said sarcastically.

"Only I needed to relieve myself, so I went behind that big tree over there, and that's when I noticed the body!"

"Anything else you noticed Mr." she said cutting herself off.

"No, no I didn't, and my names Maltby, Sid Maltby."

"Ok Mr Sid Maltby, are you sure you didn't see anything else?"

"Positive."

"Ok just jot your mobile number down for me, and then if we need to contact you again."

The workman searched frantically for a scrap piece of paper from inside his van. He opened his glove compartment, and emptied half of its contents onto his passenger's side seat. But couldn't find any kind of scrap paper. Abbot rolled her eyes impatiently. Then the workman managed to find an out-of-date till receipt. He found a chewed-up writing pen, then jotted his mobile down quickly. Handing it over to Abbot.

"Are you capable of driving home, Mr Maltby?" she asked concerned.

"Yes, I'll be fine" he said winding his window back up.

Both detectives started to walk back to Abbot's car. Peter's looked back at the workman's van as he started up the engine.

Thick black smoke bellowed out of its exhaust pipe.

"So, if you are going tonight, what will you wear?" he asked still soaking wet as he tried changing the subject.

"Ok Sergeant let's just concentrate on one thing at a time, shall we?" she said irritated.

"I'm just getting excited that's all" he chuckled.

"Well don't, we've now got two murders on our hands, and we're no further forward in solving it than the first one, in fact this is blowing right into our budget you know; Green from upstairs doesn't know yet about this other murder.

"Wait till he knows there's been another one!" muttered Peter's.

"Exactly" she said opening her car door.

She turned the key in the ignition as they both sat for a few long minutes with the engine running trying to get warm. She delved into her shoulder bag and produced a cigarette. She lit it, then blew out a plume of smoke. She turned on the wash wipers to full speed. As the rain started to fall down hard again. Peter's sat there impatiently trying to dry his hair through the heater vents.

She felt inside her coat pocket then bought out the red notebook. She quickly flicked through it again. But nothing of any importance jumped out at her until she turned to the very back page. She noticed a set of times and dates scribbled in black ink. This was the only page written on.

"Nothing much of interest in here, only a few dates and times on the back page, what do you make of it?" she said passing it over to him.

He reached out his hand and took it off her whilst trying to straighten his hair with his left hand.

He looked down at the scribbled letters and numbers.

"Well, whatever they are the dates only start from the fourth of this month" he suggested frowning.

"Yes, but last night he got murdered, on the eighth."

She peered over his shoulder, then leaned hard against the leather headrest. She rolled down her window, then blew out a plume of smoke. She sat deep in thought for a long second.

"I wonder what our mystery man was up to, I bet he was on to something by way of watching someone's coming and goings?" she said absently.

"Yeah, but who, and why?" he said handing the notebook back over to her.

"Well how the hell should I know, I'm just thinking out loud, aren't I?"

"Ok grumpy."

"Anyway, you're not much help, are you?" she said turning to look at him.

"No, that's because I'm soaking wet and freezing" he said shivering putting his hands up against the heater vents.

"Oh, that reminds me, I forgot to ask the doc, if there was anything else in his pockets?" she said rolling her eyes.

"Well, he's still over there, go and ask him" he said turning the heater vent setting button to full heat.

"And why don't you go and ask him, you're already soaking wet?" she said smiling at him.

He gave her a blank look. He turned away in disgust to look out his rain drenched car window.

"I know what I'll do" she said thoughtfully.

She half turned in her seat. Then reached over pulling out her mobile phone from her shoulder bag from off the back seat.

"So, what are you going to do?" he asked frowning turning back at her.

"Phoning the doc" she said punching in the Doctor's number.

"Your unbelievable you are" he said shaking his head in disbelief.

She rested the telephone against her ear, then after a couple of rings the Doctors familiar voice echoed down the line.

"Ahh, doc glad I got hold of you before you left, was there anything else in the victims' pockets?"

"Really, how interesting doc, thank you" she said ending the call.

She smiled to herself, as she put the telephone onto her lap.

"Well?" asked Peter's impatiently.

"He's just found a library card in his back pocket, in the name of Paul Andrews."

The wash wipers started to squeak and scrape across the windscreen as the rain had started to slow down again. She radioed back to the station. She reached down by the side of her gear lever and picked up the police radio. Whilst she was radioing back to the station, and between the sound of static. Peters looked down in the footwell next to his feet and found a RunRig CD amongst a load of empty screwed up crisp and sweet wrappers. He flipped it over to reveal the albums cover. It read *"In Search of Angels."*

"I've never heard of them, are they any good?" he asked frowning.

"Yes, they're a Scottish Celtic rock folk band from the Isle of Skye. They formed in nineteen seventy-three, and they're live concerts are amazing, and electric" she said replacing the police radio into its cradle.

He looked deep in thought as he scrolled down the album list. He crunched up his face, as he turned the CD back over to the front cover.

"That's where me and Richard met, at a RunRig concert, in the Barrowlands in Glasgow.

""What's it like there?" he asked frowning.

"It's like a big dance hall, all as I can remember, I went with a friend and after a lot of dancing, screaming, and shouting, Richard turned around to me from in the crowd and asked if I could stop shouting down his ears. Then after the concert I went and apologized to him, then he asked me if I wanted to go and find a bar and have a drink."

"And did you?"

"Yeah, and then everything went from there" she said smiling to herself.

She took the CD out of its case and popped it into the disc player. Then after a few long seconds the music started to come through the speakers. She turned up the volume slightly.

"Yeah, they're not bad, are they, quite like the sound of them, might stream them onto my MP3 player?" he said raising his voice over the music.

She stretched out her hand to turn down the volume as the police radio crackled through. A WPC's voice sounded on the other end.

"The name you're after Ma'am, has just come out of prison two months ago, he got sixteen years for doing a bank job in Reading."

She listened intently at the background music trying to catch every word the WPC was saying as more static, and crackling interfered with her concentration.

"His only known address is 42, Shanklin Lane" the WPC added.

"Ok, WPC, let's go and have a wee look then, shall we Sergeant?" she said wrapping her seatbelt around her. She engaged the car into gear. Peter's jolted back into his seat as she drove off at speed. He quickly grabbed his seatbelt wrapping it around him. The view from the car's window passed him at speed. They turned off the main road, and down into aside road, pulling up at the appointed address. On the front of the two-storey semi a 'TO LET' board sat above the front door. From the outside the house looked large in the tree lined street. Expensive cars parked untidily in the road.

"Looks like you need money to live down a street like this, I couldn't afford to live here" he said unhooking his seatbelt.

They both casually alighted the car and looked up at the property in question. They both slammed their car doors shut behind them. In fact, Abbot's car looked out of place.

They both walked briskly to the front iron gate, as Abbot opened it, it squeaked and clanged shut behind them both. Abbot rang the doorbell. Then after a few long seconds, the front door was finally opened a jar by a middle-aged grey-haired man.

"All the rooms are let" he grumbled.

"We haven't come about a room, we're here about one of your tenants, you've got residing here!" she said showing him her warrant card.

"Everything's all above board here, you can contact the Local Authorities if you don't believe me" he said firmly.

"We're not interested in any Local Authorities, Sir, we just need to have a wee chat that's all, may we come in?" she asked firmly.

The man opened the door wider and breathed in slightly letting them both through. He shut the door behind them as all three stood just inside the hallway.

"Which tenant are you talking about?" the man growled.

"A man called Paul Andrews" she said with her eyes darting around the confined space.

"Oh him, when you see him, tell him he still owes me a month's rent?" he snarled.

"Do you happen to have a spare key for his room, just so we can have a look around?"

"Why?" the man growled.

"We promise we won't disturb anything?" said Peter's ignoring his question.

The man squeezed passed them both. Abbot heard him muttering something under his breath. He encouraged both detectives to follow him up the narrow staircase. It led them all down a narrow corridor until they reached the particular room.

The man delved deep inside his trouser pocket producing a set of keys. The man nervously held the key between his thumb and forefinger, placing it in the lock. He turned the key in the lock.

The hinges on the door squeaked as he opened it slowly. He stepped back into the corridor letting go of the door. Both detectives entered inside as the man still held onto the set of keys.

Once both inside. A narrow hallway led them into a small kitchenette, with a small living space that housed just a single chair and coffee table.

Just to the right of that was a cramped shower room. With a separate toilet area.

The small living space had no personal feel to it. No pictures hung on any of the surrounding walls. In fact, very little personal effects, and belongings either. Nothing to suggest anyone was even staying here.

A clock radio sat on a tiny table that was acting as a bedside draw kept flashing "ON" and "OFF" the wrong time. Even the single bed didn't look like it had been slept in.

She opened the draw with the clock radio on. Hoping to find something inside.

"Empty" she said looking at Peter's disappointingly.

She wondered over to the wardrobe that stood in the corner of the room. By the looks of it the door hadn't been opened in months. She managed to prize it open. But empty again. Not even a suitcase. She turned her attention back to the single bed. She playfully tested the mattress with both hands.

Then she pulled back the sheets and pillows then lifted up the edges of the mattress.

"Nothing there either!" she muttered.

Peter's picked up the clock radio out of desperation. There he spotted a small photograph facing up side down.

"Here, take a look at this?" he said passing it over to her.

"Well, well" she said looking down at the photograph.

In the photograph it showed two adult men in the foreground smiling down the camera lens. One being Paul Andrews.

The other man smiling back up at them was the dead tramp who was killed two nights ago.

In the background two other adult figures were laughing and enjoying themselves at what looked like a garden party.

Also, in the photograph, the sun shone bright with no cloud insight. Abbot walked back to the man still standing in the corridor.

"Excuse me Sir, do you happen to know who this man is?"

She went and stood next to him and pointed out the man in the photograph. He frowned for a long second, as though deep in thought.

"Yeah, that's his brother, Matthew Andrews" he said confidently.

She wondered back into the confined room looking for Peter's. The man followed her into the room. Then she finally found Peter's in the toilet.

"Can't a man have any kind of privacy?" he asked flushing the chain.

"Couldn't you have shut the door behind you?" she asked turning away.

"I thought you'd gone back downstairs?"

"Well, we now know who our dead tramp is?" she said ignoring his question.

She bagged up the photograph in a clear evidence bag and stood watching Peter's pulling up his trouser zip. She turned back towards the man.

"Ehh, you don't know what he did with all his belongings do you?" she asked the man curiously.

"He didn't have any when he arrived" he said walking back into the corridor.

All three headed back downstairs. Peter's was still putting his shirt in his trousers, as he descended the stairs. Abbot rolled her eyes at him in frustration.

"Thank you for letting us look around, you've been most helpful. Good day to you, Sir."

The man headed for the door. Swinging it right open. As the two detectives exited the door, Abbot gave the man a reassuring smile. He forced out a smile whilst still holding the front door open.

As the two detectives headed towards the iron gate, the man shouted.

"Oh, and don't forget, when you see Andrews, tell him about his rent?"

The two detectives stopped in their tracks and turned on their heels. Abbot walked back towards the man still holding the door wide open. She got closer, then whispered.

"I don't think he'll be paying it again; he was murdered last night!" she said turning back towards the gate. The man's pure white face changed to an unusual bright red.

After closing the iron gate behind her. She unlocked her car then the two detectives slid inside. She sighed deeply as she wrapped her seatbelt around her.

"Come on Sergeant, I need a coffee" she said turning the key in the ignition.

She pulled away from the kerbside, glancing in her rear-view mirror as she changed up a gear. Again, Peter's jolted back into his seat from the speed she set off.

"How did you ever pass your test?"

"I don't know myself to be honest" she said changing up another gear.

Chapter 12

They managed to find a seat in the window of a small, quaint cafe called "THE COFFEE BEAN" on Shanklin's main road into town which, at this time of day was pretty good considering all the school traffic.

They both enjoyed a large hot chocolate, which overflowed with marshmallows and fresh cream.

Peter's was not yet dry. He was starting to smell like a stale dog.

"I hope you're not going to smell and look like that tonight?" she said moving away from him slightly.

"No, not that it's any of your business. I'll be finishing early tonight, I'm getting my hair trimmed, and I want to try out my new aftershave."

"Oh right" she said taking a sip of chocolate.

"Anyway, I've been asked out by someone, so I don't have to try to pull tonight" he said confidently.

"The only thing you'll be pulling tonight with that

smell, is a stray cat!" she said trying not to laugh.

"Your only jealous" he said from behind his mug.

"Anyway, what's it called, your new aftershave, 'Wet Dog Potion'?" she asked bursting out laughing.

"Ha, ha, very funny" he said not very amused placing his mug back onto the table.

Later that afternoon, and back at the station the two detectives were trying to put clues together as to why Paul Andrews had a notepad with dates and times scribbled down. Also, how his brother ended up being a tramp. She leaned back into her high-backed chair whilst folding her arms together.

"I tell you what Peter's, get on the phone to Reading Police Station, and ask if they can fax over the case file for the night of the bank job, see if we can find anything?" she suggested frowning at him.

He rose to his feet and headed for the door. After a couple of long minutes, he re-entered her office with a smile on his face.

"They'll fax it over first thing tomorrow morning for you" he said sitting down opposite her again.

"Ok Sergeant, thank you" she said distantly still looking at the notepad.

"What's the matter?" he inquired frowning.

"Oh, it's nothing, just thinking that's all."

"You sure that's a good idea?" he said winking at her.

He rose to his feet again, heading for the door. He pulled down hard on the door handle, with a big smile on his face.

"And where do you think you're going?"

"I'm going home to get ready for the big night tonight" he said still smiling.

"But we've got work to do?"

"You might have, but I'm going to have some fun tonight, and let my hair down!"

"How can you let your hair down if you're having it trimmed you fool?" she said patronizingly.

"At least I'm going with someone" he said shutting the door behind him.

Later that night, Abbot changed out of her tight blue jeans and woolly jumper. She looked a stunner. She wore her hair up in big queen beauty style. With a short black dress. She also wore black tights and high heeled shoes. Over her left shoulder hung a black bag with gold chains, bearing the hallmarks of Gucci. She slowly headed over towards the bar.

The barman wiped down the counter with his white cloth as he asked her what she wanted.

"Gin and tonic?"

It looked like the party was already in full swing. It was a good turnout considering. Abbot thought many of the detectives just wanted to let their hair down and have a good time tonight, and why not, they've all worked hard.

She saw Peter's walking in with the young WPC holding onto his arm. They stepped down two steps to the same level as the dancing floor. Abbot felt lost and alone. She wished she had someone to have and to hold for the night.

"Blimey, that didn't take him long?" she thought to herself, looking in Peter's direction.

Peter's spotted Abbot standing alone at the bar. He quickly rushed the young WPC to a nearby table, at the other end of the room. He casually walked over to Abbot. Smiling from ear to ear.

"Oh yeah, don't tell me it's your new aftershave couldn't she resist" she said shouting over the sudden sound of loud music.

"Not really, she's been badgering me all week to bring her, I couldn't let her down, could I?" he said leaning against the bar.

"She looks very pretty out of uniform, what's her name?" she asked discreetly looking over his shoulder.

"I just know her as WPC Grange" he said sounding embarrassed.

The barman kept on ignoring Peter's as he leaned his elbows along the counter.

"Well, you won't get very far with just WPC Grange, will you?" she said poking him in the ribs.

"Ehh, barman?" he shouted.

He tried getting the barman's attention by stretching out his arm. But for some reason, it still didn't work.

"What's her first name, dope?" she asked taking a sip of her drink.

"Ehh, no idea" he said still trying to get the barman's attention.

"What you going to tell her when you have to be back home by eleven o'clock, or will your landlady lock you out do you think?" she said smiling enjoying the teasing.

"All I'm asking is for a drink" he shouted over the sound of music.

"Now, look here, I don't have to put up with your attitude" said the barman walking off rolling his eyes.

"You better take her a drink over, and have a dance with her, you'll have to leave soon."

"If I could ever get one" he said watching the barman disappear into the distance.

"Well, why don't you ask for one then?"

"Leave it out will you."

"I'm only saying" she said trying not to laugh.

"I'm going to have a good night, so if you don't mind, you're cramping my style" he growled.

"Cramping your style, you better be on your toes tonight then, you might get lucky?"

He walked away from the bar still empty handed with no drinks. He walked confidently over the dancing floor, heading back to WPC Grange.

Later as the night wore on, Abbot was still sitting at the bar on her own. The odd off-duty detective flocked around her to see how far they might get by means of chatting her up. Only to find out it was completely useless. She was shooting them down time after time. Before long Peter's returned and sat next to her.

"Can I join you?" he asked shyly.

"Cause you can, where's the young WPC, whatever her name is?" she asked putting her glass to her mouth.

"Oh, she's gone off and left me, she's holding one of the off-duty detectives' hands over there."

"Did you tell her you had to get home early?"

"Oh right."

"I just don't think she likes me, that's all after I bought her a drink as well" he said sounding disappointed.

"Oh, you managed to get a drink then?"

"Yes."

"If you only bought her the one drink, no wonder she's gone off with someone else?" she said laughing.

"I'm skint this month, I couldn't tell her that, could I, or she wouldn't have wanted to come out with me?" he said embarrassed.

"Men really are completely incapable!" she said beckoning the barman back over.

"What you having Peter's, it's on me?" she asked smiling.

"I'll have a pint of your best please, barman" he said with a reassuring smile at him.

"And I'll have another Gin and Tonic" she said placing her empty glass back down on the counter.

After a few more alcoholic drinks Peter's was feeling

a little tipsy. The room started spinning. But the noise from the loud music was just a repetitive beating sound. Abbot crunched up her face and moved closer into Peter's shoulders. She could smell his cheap lingering aftershave. She was right. It did smell of stale dogs!

"It's not actually a bad night is it, Peter's?" she said shouting down his ear.

"Have you seen Jones yet?"

"What?" he shouted putting his hand against his ear, in order to hear.

They both turned round on their bar stools to face the crowd. Jones was in the middle of the room dancing away with a red party hat on his head. He was drinking with the young WPC Grange.

"Oh, look isn't that your young WPC friend?" she suggested glancing over.

"The way he's been knocking them back, I'm surprised he's still standing" he growled with jealousy.

"It's a good job, because now he's sitting down" she commented dryly.

"Oh, you don't have to be so precise, do you?" he said gloomily.

He glanced back towards Abbot. Then put his empty glass on the counter. He had a feeling of nervousness suddenly come over him. But he knew he had to tell her about his feelings from the other night. He moved in a little closer. He could smell her sweet perfume as he still glared at her. He paused for a long second. He needed to do this.

"Look Karen, about the other night…" he said cutting himself off.

She cut off his conversation by putting her hand up to his face. She knew by the tone of his voice, what was coming next. He only used her first name when he felt uncomfortable.

"I don't want to talk about it, it was a stupid mistake, and it shouldn't have happened."

"Will you shut up for a minute will you" he said gritting his teeth.

He staggered to his feet from off the bar stool. Then slipped his hands in his trouser pockets. As he usually does when he's nervous.

"It may not have meant anything to you, but it certainly did to me."

"Oh."

"Look, I like you a lot and I know you and Richard are having difficulties between you both and I just wanted to tell you how I feel, before I go to the mainland that's all, I've always fancied you, ever since I was assigned to work with you all those years ago, you're pretty and your fun to be around, you're outgoing, and you know, I've got to say, Richards a very lucky man."

"Don't be daft, it's the drink talking" she said looking down at the floor.

She reached into her shoulder bag and produced a box of cigarettes. She held it between her thumb and index finger, then lit it.

"You're right, Richard is a very lucky man, but he's blown it" she said blowing out a plume of smoke whispering in his ear.

"Blown it, what do you mean?" he asked frowning.

"He's gone and traded me in for another model" she said blowing out another plume of smoke.

"The unfaithful swine" he said angrily.

He looked deep into her dark brown eyes. They glistened with emotion in the disco lights.

"How long have you known?"

"No idea, it's the woman who's got a son in my daughter's class."

She stopped talking for a long minute, turning back towards the barman to ask for another alcoholic drink. Then she turned back to Peter's and leaned into his chest.

"Look, the other night."

"I know what you're going to say, you've already said it."

"Have I?" she asked frowning.

"In no certain terms."

"It was nice to make me feel like a woman again, I'd forgotten what that felt like, and it was certainly nice to feel alive again so why don't you go and find that nice young WPC friend of yours that you came in with, before it's too late and go and make her feel like a woman" she said whispering in his ear.

His eyes narrowed as he gave her a reassuring smile. He took his hands out his pockets, then staggered off towards the dancing floor to go and find WPC Grange.

Chapter 13

Reading police station had faxed over the case notes of Paul and Matthew Andrews. They sat in a pile on her desk. Which had a scribbled handwritten note attached on the front of it which read: "URGENT."

Abbot walked into her office holding her forehead from last night's party. She put down her shoulder bag at the side of her desk. She pulled out her high-backed chair from under her chair, then noticed the case notes immediately. She opened the file open wide and started to read its contents. Halfway through reading the contents she lifted her desk telephone receiver and placed it against her ear. She flicked her hair behind her left ear, as she dialed Peter's extension number to his desk. After a couple of rings, his familiar voice echoed down the line.

"Yes, what is it?" he asked looking up into her office window.

"Have you got a minute Sergeant?" she said ending the call.

She replaced the telephone receiver back into its cradle, next to a photograph of her and Richard laughing down the camera lens. Peter's knocked gently on her office door.

He'd got regrets about the party last night. He'd had a couple of drinks too many and had said a few things that he should have kept to himself. He told himself off, before he reached her office.

He opened the door, and went in. She was still sifting through the case notes when he closed the door behind him.

He didn't bother looking at her beauty as he pulled up a chair opposite her desk. She stopped reading for a second, then sighed as she leaned back into her chair.

"I've just been reading through these case notes, and something doesn't add up" she said still looking down at the case notes.

"Like what?" he asked frowning.

"Well, I don't know, I can't work it out, there's something not right here. I just can't put my finger on it" she said finally looking up at him.

"Let me have a look" he said reaching over her desk.

"How did you get on last night with the young WPC?" she asked curiously changing the subject.

"Oh that, not very good, she ended up going home with someone else" he said disappointingly.

"Never mind Peter's, better luck next time" she said trying not to laugh.

"Anyway, when I got home about twelve thirty the landlady had only bolted the door hadn't she, so I had to climb in through the outside toilet window."

"You got to be kidding me" she said with a chuckle.

"Next thing I know, I'm having my collar felt by one of our lot, they thought I was the gang that was doing all the house break-ins, you know, the ones you've been working on."

"I bet it made their night, when they thought they'd caught someone, and it turned out to be a Sergeant from their own station" she said sounding surprised.

"It's not funny, the landlady wants me out, she said it upset her dog, that much she had to sit up with it all night, she said she doesn't want any troublemakers living there!"

"Did you happen to tell her you're an officer of the law?" she suggested firmly.

"Yeah, but she didn't believe me, she said my eyes were to close together."

"You know, I told Richard to go and find somewhere else to live last week, I can't live with all the arguments anymore."

"What did he say to that?" he said trying to hide his curiosity.

"He didn't" she said pulling a face.

"Well, I'm sorry that's happened, and I'm here for you if you want anything" he said with a reassuring smile.

"Thank you, Sergeant, I appreciate that, but I'll be ok, anyway you'll be moving to the mainland soon" she said smiling back.

"Yes, but not for another week or so."

"But before you do move away, let's see if we can crack this case hey?" she said reassuringly.

Later that morning in the briefing room. Abbot placed three enlarged photographs of the dead tramp and Paul Andrews on the whiteboard in front of her. She took a step back and held their gaze from the photographs.

Behind her came the clatter of computer keyboards being slapped down hard by a few hungover detectives.

'What's the connection?" she thought out loud before walking over to Peter's desk.

"You got a minute?" she asked again.

"Yeah, what is it?"

"I don't know yet" she said as they both walked over to the whiteboard.

"Tell me what you see?"

"What do you mean?" he asked frowning.

"Just tell me what you see in the photograph?" she said firmly.

"Ok, I see two men laughing and hugging each other with a bottle of beer in their hands."

"Ok, what else?" she said interrupting his flow of thought.

"Some people in the background sitting down talking, too far away to see who they are, no idea what year it's taken, no, I can't see anything else, I'm afraid, what should I be looking for?" he said squinting with his face right up against the whiteboard.

"I don't know, I just wanted to see if you saw anything different to what I was looking at and as for the year it was taken in 1997."

"And how can you be so sure of that?" he asked curiously studying the photographs again for clues.

"Because the year was written on the back, with a very faint pencil."

Peters tutted and walked away.

"I thought you needed my help?" he said walking away from her.

He stopped suddenly in his tracks as she followed him to his desk. He turned on his heels and crunched up his face as he carried on walking to his desk. Then leaned on the edge of it.

"I do, I'm going to get you a photocopy of the case notes, and if you Peter's would be so kind enough to look through them tonight, it would be much appreciated" she whispered.

"And, what you going to do?" he asked sarcastically.

"I'll take a copy home as well" she said patting him on the back walking back to her own office.

Later that night after everything was washed and put away. She sat at the kitchen table looking through the case files. All she could hear was the ticking from the wall clock. The house was so quiet and empty. No sound from the children as they were at Abbot's mothers again. This was becoming a regular occurrence. She felt so alone, and lonely in her own company. But it was certainly better than frequent arguments and worthless conversations of late with Richard.

She stopped for a second and raised herself from her chair to get a bottle of her favourite white wine from the fridge. She opened the fridge door wide and reached inside.

"No, not tonight girl, you need your head for this case" she said aloud to herself. She let go of the bottle.

She slammed the fridge door shut, then turned and flicked the switch for the kettle instead. She sat back down whilst the kettle boiled. She re-read them quickly once more.

'On the 10th of April 1997, at twelve thirty am a masked robber with a shotgun entered the front entrance of the Provincial Bank in Reading High Street. After forcing all the customers down onto the ground, he demanded the cashier put as much money into his rucksack as she could. If she did this no one would get hurt. His gun was loaded, he said, and he would shoot if his demands weren't met. Throughout this time, he kept the gun pointed at the Bank Manager. The ordeal was over in three minutes. She shook her head whilst still reading the notes.

(STATEMENT NUMBER 1.)

"A witness didn't get a look at the robber, but where she lay on the floor, she could see the getaway driver" she questioned this point loudly to herself."

After seeing a Photofit of the man she correctly identified him as Mr Paul Andrews. She couldn't describe the car apart from saying it was red and got four doors and a registration number. The robber wore a black mask, white running shoes and blue jeans, he also wore a combat jacket with a hole in the right-side sleeve.

I'm the Assistant Bank Manager of the Provincial Bank and was held at gun point by the robber. I didn't get much of a look as I couldn't see his face because he wore a black ski mask. I could only see his eyes, blue eyes, blue piercing eyes. I noticed he had a gold ring and a gold expensive watch; he wasn't wearing any gloves. I put the money into his rucksack bag as he ordered me to. I am not sure how much he got away with; the thing is if he had come in that afternoon there would have been more money in the tills. Funny thing was it didn't feel real, I mean it didn't look like it does on the telly. The robber seemed more interested in watching the Bank Manager than what I was doing, so that's when I pressed the panic button under my counter.

Abbot stretched her legs as she poured her hot tea. Her head was aching reading through so many notes. But she knew she had to persevere.

There was something she couldn't put her finger on. But there was definitely something. She settled herself back at the table. And started reading again.

(STATEMENT NUMBER 2.)

"I was just drawing some money out from the cash machine, which was just inside the bank, by the front door. I went inside because it was chucking it down with rain, well I'm just getting over a cold, so I didn't want to get soaked, plus I didn't have my brolly with me. I was standing by the front door when this man came bursting in and he told us all to get down on the floor and not to say a word."

"Well, my nose starts running doesn't it, well I needed my handkerchief, but it was in my trouser pocket. I didn't know what to do so I just left it to run. Looking back now, when he did burst in waving his gun around, it looked like he was looking for someone, it looked like he wasn't sure what he was doing like, you know what I mean."

"When I saw the red car revving the engine hard, I thought that doesn't sound right, it sounded like it needed new tappets or some oil or something. I didn't realise he was waiting for someone to come out the bank, well when the bloke with the mask came running out, I didn't know what to think, well you don't do you, these days."

(STATEMENT NUMBER 3.)

"I was sitting having a latte minding my own business when this man sat in a red car across the road from the café started revving the engine, noisy it was. I told the girl in the cafe to phone the police, making all that racket and when he drove off, well, it's a good job nobody was in his way. Wheels were screeching, the poor man who got into the car didn't have time to take his hat off or put his seatbelt on."

"I can't take anymore of this twaddle anymore, I need something stronger than coffee now" she said aloud.

She looked up at the wall clock which read 12.30pm. She looked down in frustration at the case files. She felt she needed some company.

"I can't phone Peter's now, it's far too late, plus I don't think his landlady would be too pleased if I phoned him at this late hour" she said aloud to herself again.

She searched for her car keys under the piles of paperwork on the table. She couldn't find them so, she shuffled around into her coat pocket.

"Where the hell are they?"

She searched frantically through her shoulder bag sending tissues and lipstick flying all over the floor.

"They can't be far away, I drove home, I'm going as mad as them witnesses, talking to myself."

She finally found them hidden inside the folded flap of the case notes file.

"Why am I talking to myself?" she muttered to herself again.

Soon she was driving through the quiet and deserted streets of Shanklin. She found herself at a fork in the road. She stopped at the junction, then indicated right. The dark country lane she'd turned onto was nothing more than for slow moving traffic. She didn't realise it was for farm traffic.

In the distance she could make out the bright light from the lighthouse. Cutting through the darkness of the night. Her own car headlights pierced through the eerie darkness. Catching the silhouette on the bare trees that hung low which swung in a cold and raising wind. After a few more twists and turns. She eventually arrived at Peter's address. She pulled up kerbside, then reached for a cigarette.

"What am I doing here?" she said lighting the cigarette.

She turned on the disc player in her car. Then just listened to her favourite RunRig song through the speakers.

She sat and waited until the cigarette smoldered away to nothing in her fingers. She listened to a few more songs from her favourite album. She unhooked her seatbelt, then stepped out into the cold night air. She slowly walked up the garden path and knocked on the front door.

She could hear a woman's faint voice coming from behind the door.

"Who is it, I'll phone the police?"

"I am the police" she shouted through the letter box.

"Goodness me, that was quick" said the landlady.

She opened the door in a long pink dressing gown. Her hair was tucked up all in rollers. Abbot looked down at the woman's feet. The women wore a pair of soft slippers that had pom-poms attached to them. Abbot shook her head in disbelief.

"Can I speak to Ian Peters please?" she asked now smiling at the landlady.

"You come to arrest him again, have you?"

Peter's stood at the top of the stairs looking down at the couple. All he was wearing was a pair of blue boxers.

"Oh, that's not a nice sight at this time in the morning, I'm glad I haven't just eaten" said Abbot trying not to stare.

"What's the matter anyway, it's nearly two am?" he whispered loudly scratching his head.

"Yeah, well don't worry about the time, just go and get some clothes on, we're going for a drive."

"A drive, but I'm tired" he said yawning.

"Well, I'm not, I'll be waiting in the car" she ordered walking out the front door.

A few moments later and Abbot was driving down the dark deserted lanes again. Both sat in silence until she pulled into the car park at Needles point.

They sat and watched as the deep dark sea spread out before them. The moon shone on the swirling and tossing waves crashing aimlessly against the eroding cliffs. The cars headlights broke the eeriness of the dark.

"What we doing here, it's pitch black?" he asked yawning again.

"I couldn't sleep, things were going round in my head like a washing machine" she said unhooking her seatbelt.

"I know how you feel" he muttered.

"No, I mean, my life has just turned itself around, for me this last week, I found out my husband is having an affair with our daughters friends Mum, how long it's been going on I'm not sure?" she said rolling down the window.

She glanced over at him. His hair bushy from not combing it. He stared straight ahead of him.

"We invited her to our last barbecue you know, we had this year, she got so drunk Richard had to drive her home, it could have started then I suppose, I just remembered it tonight" she said absently.

Peter's still stared straight ahead. She didn't know if he was listening to her.

"Then my oldest daughter gets into trouble with the schools Headmistress, she later tells me she doesn't want to go to college, she wants to be a copper like me, but I told her to do what I did."

She sighed deeply into the air folding her arms. She pushed her head hard against the leather headrest.

"I told her, you have to study long and hard, but she said, she'll skip college and go straight into university, and because I work long hours, they spend more time round their grandmas than they do with me."

A strong gust of wind blew around the car. Sprinklings of rain started to patter on the windscreen. She rolled her window back up.

"I've been thinking, I might quit being a detective after this case is closed, I've been doing it for far too long now, I could spend more time at home with the girls, watch Grace grow up, I don't know, maybe it's all I know, is being a copper" she said softly.

Peter's turned his head towards her.

"You could have told me all this over the phone?" he said begrudgingly looking at his wristwatch.

"But what I'm struggling with most in this case?" she said cutting herself off in mid conversation.

"Meaning?" he asked confused.

"There's a motive in these two murders somewhere, and I want to know what that is, the killer, killed them both the same way."

Peter's shrugged his shoulders tight into his chest.

"Why?"

"Why, what?" he asked absently.

"Did the killer know they were brothers, or just randomly kill them both?"

Peters shrugged his shoulders again in frustration.

"You read the statements off the witnesses yet, they all read like a comedy sketch?" she said snorting.

She reached for her cigarettes from the centre counsel. She lit the cigarette holding it between her thumb and forefinger.

"I didn't get time last night; I was putting my best belongings into bags getting ready to move" he said trying not to nod off.

She blew out a plume of smoke. Turning the key in the ignition.

"I know the killer knew his victims, he had to have known them, nine times out of ten the killer knows his victims" she said pressing the button for the wash wipers.

She rolled down the window again. This time to discard the cigarette butt. She wrapped her seatbelt around her. Peter's did the same as he knew her style of driving.

Come on sleepy head, let's get you back to bed?" she said putting the car into gear.

"That would be nice, my nice warm bed" he said closing his eyes.

She turned the car around. Then headed for the main road home.

Chapter 14

Later that morning Abbot sat in her office at her desk, with a cup of coffee in one hand and a cigarette lit in the other. Heavy-eyed and tired she watched Peter's walk over to his own desk trying not to be noticed by the other detectives in the room. He was two hours late for work.

Abbot armed with her coffee clenched in her hand, she aimed for her door. She pulled down on the door handle, opening it wide staring over in Peter's direction. He swiveled round in his chair as he noticed Abbot in her office doorway.

"Sorry, I overlay" he said raising his voice.

"Oh, don't worry about the time, just don't let Green upstairs hear you were late."

"Thank you" he said smiling at her.

"If he does ask, just tell him you were working on a hunch on this case" she said winking walking over to the briefing room. She cleared her throat with a cough, to get everyone's attention. The other group of detectives in the outer office were all busy tapping away at their computer keyboards. They stopped what they were doing, with a moan and groan. Abbot rolled her eyes discreetly into the air.

"Ok anyone, do we still have the CCTV from the bank, I need to have a look through it, at some point?"

"It's here Ma'am" said a detective from the back of the room.

He held up the video cassette in his hand, then rose to his feet to go and hand it over to her. He had to walk sideways due to how the other detectives was sitting akwardly at their desks.

She thanked the detective then looked over in Peter's direction. He was slumped at his desk holding himself up with his hands against his head.

"Peter's get me a video machine, would you?" she said clicking her fingers at him.

He staggered up out of his chair. Then walked off in the direction of the corridor. A few long moments later he wheeled in a TV and a video machine on a trolley.

"Ok plug it in Peter's, gather round everyone, let's get this case solved, it's running into our budget."

A group of detectives sat cramped around the TV screen. Abbot pressed the "PLAY" button on the remote control.

After a couple of long seconds later. A snowy picture appeared on the screen. It was hard to make out anything. The camera shot was from the top of the high street. That's all they could make out. Various unknown figures walked past the camera throughout that night in question. Abbot fast forwarded the screen. She stopped once she'd found what she was looking for two very blurred figures walked past the camera. She squinted at the snowy screen.

"Detective Jameson, did you take this to forensics to get it enhanced?" she asked still squinting.

"Yes Ma'am, that's the best they could do."

"It's not very good is it, that could be anyone and how do we know that's Matthew's walking by, ok everyone, back in your places?" she said sighing taking out the video from the machine.

All the other detectives started to move back into their places. Abbot aimed herself through the crowd to Peter's desk.

"Peter's, you got a wee minute?" she asked putting the video cassette down on his desk.

"Sure."

She reached out and picked up the video cassette again whilst Peter's muttered under his breath as he was rising to his feet. They both walked over in the direction of Abbot's office.

"Shut the door Sergeant, let's keep the heat in" she said sitting down at her desk.

He looked down at the floor as he shut the door behind him. He wondered over by the window and reached for a chair. Then he placed it opposite her desk. He sat down and crossed his legs for comfort. Abbot leaned back in her chair whilst folding her arms.

"I err just want to thank you for last night, or rather the wee hours of this morning, I'd rather no one gets to hear about it, just you and me ok Sergeant?"

"Your secrets safe with me you can count on that" he said yawning.

"Thanks, it means a lot you listening to me."

"Anytime, and you know I'll be there for you if you need anything."

"I know I can rely on you, and hope everything goes well in your new position on the mainland."

"You know really I don't want to go."

"Oh, why not?"

"I think you know why?"

"I know, and I appreciate all what you've said and done. And I just want to really say thank you for listening to my problems last night."

"Think nothing of it, it was my pleasure" he said yawning behind his hand.

"Hopefully we can do it again sometime before you leave for the mainland?" she said with emotion in her voice.

"Yes, I'd love to, but first I've just been skipping through the bank robbery notes, and funny enough, the bank managers name is the same as the one in Reading, all those years ago, it could be a coincidence, or…?" he said cutting himself off.

"What was the bank managers name in Reading?"

"Ehh a Mr Edwards."

He played with his tie, then rose to his feet walking around to Abbots side of her desk. And vigorously searched frantically through the files notes that was lying on her desk. Finally, he found the page.

"Ahh here we are, read from there, what the cashier said" he said pointing to the notes on the page.

"The robber seemed more interested in the bank manager, then what I was doing, that's when I pressed the panic button under my counter" she said reading it out loud.

"And further down?" he added pointing on the page again.

"And we have the bank managers account, I didn't get much of a look, he was the only person looking at him and why would he just keep the gun fixed on the bank manager?" he said excitedly.

"And again here, the witness said he looked like he was looking for someone, it looked like he wasn't sure what he was doing" he added as he went and sat back down.

"You don't rob a bank, go inside and look for someone, then keep your eyes fixated just on one person, you keep looking around you, to see what everyone else is doing, someone might be a hero and get up and have a go, try and get the gun or something" he said folding his arms.

Abbot frowned as she stood up then sat on the edge of her desk. One leg swinging. Peter's put a smug smile on his face.

"I reckon it could have been an inside job?" he said slipping his hands in his pockets.

"What makes you so sure Sergeant?" she asked scratching her chin.

"Look at the facts, I think it could have been a dummy run, and Matthews kept looking at Mr Edwards for reassurance, most probably because Matthews wasn't confident enough, or he was too nervous, or something."

"Yeah, and isn't it a funny coincidence the bank managers on the Isle of Wight after eighteen years, and so are the two Matthew brothers but Mr Edwards wouldn't be stupid enough to walk past his own bank with Matthews on the night of the murder surely?" she said doubtfully.

"Yes, but he knew in the morning that the tapes would be wiped clean and taped over again for the following night he could wipe the tapes clean, he's the manager, it's most probably his first job of the day, but he wasn't counting on us turning up for it asking to have a look, and if you remember, he was a little cagey about us asking to have a look, never mind taking the security tape" he said all with excitement in his voice.

"Get onto the Provincial Banks Head Office and see what happened to our Mr Edwards after the robbery, see if they can tell us anything?" she said standing up off the edge of the desk.

"Ok" he said with still excitement in his voice.

Chapter 15

Later that afternoon in the canteen. Abbot shouted in Peter's direction who was waiting to be served in the queue.

She wanted to know what progress he'd made with the banks head office.

It seemed an age before he was served, then eventually he came and sat beside her. He placed his full tray of dinner on the table in front of her. She glanced over at his plate and noticed the wisps of steam arising from his cottage pie and vegetables. She rolled her eyes at his hot food, as hers wasn't so hot! He clunked his knife and fork, then his plate onto the table from off his tray. He placed his empty tray on the chair next to him. He sat down, grating his chair along the tiled floor. He gave her a reassuring smile as he picked up his knife and fork. He glanced over to see her looking at his pile of hot steaming food.

"How did you get on with the banks head office?" she asked him in between a mouthful of mashed potato.

He took a mouthful of his steaming hot cottage pie. Abbot rolled her eyes at him again in disgust as hers was now luck warm nearly cold.

"Well, what did they tell you, or not tell you?" she asked crunching up her face as the cold potato went down the back of her throat.

He unwittingly infuriated her further as he gasped and tucked more into his hot food.

"Blimey, that was hot" he said wafting his mouth with his hand.

"I wouldn't know" she said shaking her head in disbelief.

"According to head office of the Provincial Bank, they said that Mr Edwards went for counselling shortly after the robbery and asked for a transfer" he said taking another mouthful of potato gingerly.

Abbot looked down at her plate of food. It certainly wasn't cod-en-bleu! She crunched up her face then placed the knife and fork onto the half-eaten food. She pushed the plate into the middle of the table.

"Did they say where he was transferred to?"

"Yeah, the Isle of Wight, they honed him the transfer on the grounds of shock, he was transferred here in a matter of weeks also, nobody had a bad word to say against him, he was well liked by everyone who worked with him, a role employee they said" he said putting his knife and fork down on now his empty plate.

"How do you eat hot food so quick?"

"Easy, when you're not doing the talking!"

She rolled her eyes as she stood up grating her chair along the tiled floor. She pulled in her chair under the table, then reached out for her cup of coffee. She crunched up her face in disgust. Even that was cold!

"I think we should go and have a wee word with Mr Edwards, don't you Sergeant?" she said replacing the cup back onto the table.

"What now, I was hoping to have some jam roly poly and custard before it's all gone? It looks delicious" he said slapping his lips.

"Well hurry up will you" she said sighing looking at her wristwatch.

Later, they were both soon driving through the villages and towns making twists and turns through the now with rain wet streets. Her wash wipers slapped in time to the speed of the rain. The car splashed in the puddles making waves from her tyres. Darkness was looming ahead of them, as they turned off the main road. She changed down a gear, to climb a slight incline to the road they needed. She made an immediate right without any kind of signaling for the car behind. The motorist behind sounded his horn aggressively. Peter's shook his head in disgust and hoped to be out of the moving vehicle soon. She glanced in her rear-view mirror, as she noticed the motorist behind making rude hand gestures. She pulled up her silver Volvo kerbside to the bank, clipping the kerb. Peter's shook his head again in disgust.

"What?" she asked yanking on her handbrake.

Peter's shook his head again as the wash wipers scraped along the windscreen now the rain had stopped. She'd forgotten to switch them off miles back!

"What?" she asked shrugging her shoulders.

"Haven't you realized it's not raining anymore?"

"Yes, I was wondering how long it would take you to figure that out."

"Why me, I'm not driving?"

"Because I got distracted."

"Distracted with what?"

"Do you always have to ask stupid questions?" she said unhooking her seatbelt.

Peter's unhooked his seatbelt, then they stepped out of the car into the darkening damp, cold air. Abbot looked up at the building as she locked her car behind her. They both walked into the main entrance confidently. The young bank clerk greeted them both with a false smile.

"Oh, it's you, bought our video tape back then?"

"Ehh no, we're keeping that for evidence, we just wondered if Mr Edwards was available to have a wee chat?" she asked firmly.

"I'll just phone through to his office, I know he has a four o' clock appointment" said the young woman picking up the phone receiver.

She placed the telephone receiver against her ear, then she punched in the bank managers extension number. She waited a long second. She rolled her eyes as she relayed the message in her prim and professional voice. She nodded slightly. Then replaced the receiver back into its cradle next to her computer.

"He said he'll be with you both shortly."

A couple of minutes later and Mr Edwards appeared from his office. He walked over to the two detectives with his arm outstretched. All three shook hands.

"Ahh Mr Edwards, do you have somewhere private we could have a wee chat, it won't take long?" she said drawing a false smile.

"Ehh yes in my office, I can't be too long though, I have an appointment shortly" he said directing them to his office.

Mr Edwards was determined to put on a show of authority as the two followed him into his office.

"Nice big office Mr Edwards, mine looks nothing like this" she commented on immediately.

The room was fitted out with state of the art computer equipment. The original high ceiling chandelier hung down hovering above the well-polished veneer desk. All four walls had patterned wallpaper on to make the room more inviting. Original black and white pictures of the bank hung on string coming from the picture railings around the walls.

"Head office, do look after me here I must say, I can't complain" he said puffing out his chest with pride smiling.

"Very nice" she said still looking around the room.

"Sit down won't you both" he said stretching out his arm in the direction of two leather chairs.

"We'd rather stand all the same, Sir" Peter's replied getting out his notebook.

"Now, what can I do you for?" he asked nervously sitting down at his desk.

"Well as you know Sir, we're investigating a murder that happened not too far away from here, the body was found near to the entrance of the church of All Saints, and we just wanted to know if you knew the victim his name was Paul Andrews from a town called, what was it called Peter's?" she asked turning towards Peter's.

Peter's who in turn pretended to open his notebook to a random page.

"Ehh Banbury."

"Thank you, Sergeant."

She paused again. This time glaring at the man hard. She made him look uncomfortable.

"Is any of this making any sense Mr Edwards, because my patience is wearing a wee bit thin, and when you've stopped playing silly sods, maybe we can solve this wee puzzle that I've got piling up on my ever so small desk?" she said firmly and impatiently.

"What do you want me to say, I haven't done anything wrong?" he said raising his voice at them both.

"We'll be the judge of that Mr Edwards" said Peter's firmly.

"You see you're in an old photo we have in our possession back at the nick, you were a wee bit younger back then, you were at a garden party somewhere, so this is why we have reason to believe you were involved with the bank robbery, eighteen years ago at your Reading branch, with the two men in question, oh, did I not forget to mention, that the other man we found dead in the same graveyard was the brother of Matthew Andrews he was the getaway driver" she said leaning over his desk.

The man's adams apple was moving quicker than a forklift truck.

"I don't know anyone of them names, and why should I, I don't circle with the likes of tramps?" he said nervously.

"He hasn't always been down on his luck, how he got there, we don't know, but what I'm guessing Sir, his half of the money ran out, I don't know I could be wrong" she added pacing the floor.

"What money, I don't know anything about any money?" he said adamantly.

"Well, we think you do?"

"Prove it."

"The thing is Mr Edwards, I think you were their inside man, and shortly after the robbery you got transferred to this nice new bank, not one in the next town, oh no, but on a wee island, now how does that look to us Mr Edwards?" she said turning back towards him.

"The bank believed you of course, you'd been with them for years, you get a third of the money and then start a new life, over here, no one would suspect a thing, the bank would write the money off as an insurance loss, and you'd keep the money, am I right Sir?" she said with a false smile.

"I told you I don't know anybody called Andrews and I don't know about any money" he said quivering.

"I've been wanting to say this for ages, get your coat, you're nicked."

"What for?"

"We've just told you why, aren't you listening?"

The bank manager stooped his head towards the wooden polished floor in shame. Abbot looked over at Peter's and gave him a reassuring smile. He could see her eyes glisten in the light of the overhanging chandelier above all three of them.

Chapter 16

Later at the station in the interview room. Mr Edwards sat opposite Abbot on a plastic chair. She pressed the button on the tape-recording machine. She studied his facial expressions whilst the machine was waiting to begin. She wondered how this nervous looking man would cope in prison. Not that Abbot showed much sympathy, but just wondered anyway. She looked over her right shoulder at Peter's, who was armed with a pen and notebook he had some questions of his own to ask. The recording machine seemed to take an age to start. Abbot leaned back in her chair then folded her arms tight into her chest. Mr Edwards looked uncomfortable and started to fidget in his chair. He looked up from the graffitied table and stared at both detectives. Finally, the recording machine stopped buzzing.

"For the benefit of the tape Detective Sergeant Karen Abbot, and Sergeant Ian Peter's are present to interview Mr Edwards at fourteen twenty five pm" she said checking her wristwatch.

"Ok Mr Edwards, do you know why you are here, and do you want a lawyer present?" suggested Peter's.

"Yes, I do, and no let's just get it over with" the man said softly.

"Ok, in your own words, tell us what happened" Peter's asked folding his arms.

The man sat upright in his chair and paused for a long second. Sweat was starting to appear on his forehead. He reached out, and placed both hands on the table, clasping them together tightly.

"I remember me and Paul, sat down one day and got chatting about things, one thing led to another, he asked me if my bank had ever been robbed? I told him that my bank had never been robbed. Then he asked would I be interested in making some money. Well, I didn't like where this conversation was going, so I tried changing the subject, but he kept going on about it, then he told me that he'd thought about doing a bank job for years? I didn't know what to say" he said unclasping his sweaty hands.

"So, what did you say?" inquired Peter's curiously.

"As the night went on, and we had a few more beers. He came up and asked me the same question. Well, this time I agreed, he suggested that I'd get a good cut for all my efforts he said I wouldn't have to do much for the money. I was still hesitant about the whole thing. So, we arranged the following night to meet up in a local pub to discuss how and when it was going to be done."

"And how was it going to be done?" asked Abbot with her arms still folded.

"We met at the pub the following night as arranged sitting at the back out of everyone's way then the two brothers were going to decide who was going to do what?"

"What do you mean?" asked Peter's frowning.

"Well, who was going to do the bank, and who was going to drive the getaway car, that sort of thing?"

"Whose car were they going to use?" asked Peter's straightening his tie.

"None of them had a car, what they were going to do was going to steal a car the night before from Oxford."

"What happened after that?" asked Peter's again.

"After the job, Paul burnt it out on some wasteland somewhere."

"Do you know where?"

"No, he didn't say."

"So how did they get to Oxford, from Banbury without a car, in the first place?" suggested Abbot unfolding her arms.

"They got a train, waited till nightfall, then stole one from a supermarket car park."

"Then what happened?" she asked leaning forward.

"On the day we'd scheduled the robbery, Matthew was getting cold feet, he didn't want to go through with it so Paul rang me about eleven o'clock pretending to be a customer, asking about his overdraft then he suggested to me it might be off, so I didn't really know if it was on or off?"

"So how did you know the job was going to be on?"

"I didn't until about twelve thirty pm he came charging into the bank with a revolver."

"Then what happened?" asked Peter's looking down at his scribbled notes.

"The fool kept the revolver pointing towards my face."

"Ok, did you think he was capable of using it?" she asked thoughtfully.

"Who knows, I didn't want to risk it did I?" he said sighing deeply.

"How much do you think you all got away with?" she asked holding his gaze.

"I don't know exactly, maybe one hundred thousand" he said frowning as to remember.

"Back then that was a lot of money" said Peter's writing down the figure.

"You're telling me" the man said softly.

"Did you happen to get your share of the money?"

"Every penny" said the man swallowing hard.

"Ok, how long did it take to get your share of the money?" said Peter's crunching up his face.

"Before the job we'd arranged to meet at my allotment, nobody goes up there after dark. I had a plot up there with a small shed, so we knew we were safe."

"What happened while you were there?"

"We split the money three ways, had a laugh, a drink to celebrate, then went our separate ways. I acted all innocent, and kept my job, and got a transfer in the bargain" he said leaning back in his chair.

"So, what happened to the two brothers?" she asked curiously.

Before he had time to answer the question, a faint knock at the door was heard. Abbot rolled her eyes into the air.

"Come in."

A uniformed Constable opened the door with both hands full with a tray of steaming hot tea.

He headed towards the three figures sitting at the bolted down table.

"For the benefit of the tape, Constable Jameson enters the room" she said watching him placing the tray onto the table.

The Constable looked uncomfortable taking three cups of tea from off his tray putting them down in front of all three figures. All three figures looked up at the Constable as he tried to do the task quickly. Then he turned on his heals heading towards the door. Abbot picks up her steaming hot tea, then blows away the whisps of steam. She takes a sip, then replaces the cup back on the table. Then looks up at the man staring down into his hot cup of tea.

"So, what happened to the two brothers?" she asked for a second time.

"I don't know, we went our separate ways, and we left it at that" he said picking up his polystyrene cup.

"So, what happened next?"

"I read in the papers that Paul got caught, the daft sod, went and tried doing a post office, trust him to go where they got security guards on the doors" he said replacing his cup on the table.

"Did you think he was that stupid?" asked Abbot folding her arms again.

"Well, he got away with it the first time around."

"Why do you think he wanted to do a post office?" asked Peter's holding his gaze.

"I don't know really, luck I suppose."

"So, do you know how Matthew came to be down on his luck?" asked Peter's scribbling down what the manager said.

"I think he gambled, and drank it away, he couldn't handle it."

"What do you think made him start drinking and gambling?"

"All the money he made from the bank job."

"Did Matthew have any family?" asked Peter's taking a sip of tea.

"He did have a lovely wife and a beautiful young daughter, when I used to go and visit."

"Did have?" Abbot inquired frowning.

"Yeah, I think she kicked him out, by all accounts, she'd had enough of him coming home drunk every night, I don't

131

know where they are now, it's been eighteen years since I've seen them."

"We'll have to try and locate them and inform them of his death" said Peter's taking another sip of tea.

"So, what did you do with your money?" inquired Abbot.

"We, I mean me, and the wife went on expensive holidays, bought a new car, had an extension on the new house" he said taking another gulp of tea.

"Did, your wife know what you were planning on doing?" asked Peter's toying with his pen.

"No, we kept it to ourselves."

"Did anybody else know about what you were planning to do?"

"No, nobody" he said firmly.

"Did you ever tell your wife, at any time that you were involved in the bank job?"

"Goodness me no, I got home that night, and I told her that there had been a robbery at the bank."

"Is that all you told her?"

"Yes, then a week or so later I was told about a transfer, then I told her about it, she was excited of the fact we were going to the Isle of Wight, like I said head office had no idea I was involved."

"So, why did you kill Paul and Matthew Andrews?" she asked leaning back in her chair whilst folding her arms.

"I had to do something."

"Yeah, but not by means of killing, did you have a fall out over the money, or do you think he was planning on doing another job on your bank, you see we've got evidence of a written nature to suggest otherwise Mr Edwards?" she said patronizingly.

"I don't know anything about the evidence of any written nature" he said shaking his head.

"You've done it once before, it could be done again, no one would suspect you after twenty years, it would look like just another bank robbery" suggested Peter's straightening his tie.

"No, it was nothing like that" the man said aggressively.

"Well, what was it like then Mr Edwards?" Abbot asked impatiently.

"They were going to inform the police, and the banks head office about my involvement in the robbery, if I didn't give them any money, they were going to tell the newspapers as well" he said bowing his head down.

"So, they were trying to blackmail you?"

"They told me to draw out small amounts of cash from customers bank accounts, they said that a small amount of money, no one would ever suspect it and notice it disappearing from their accounts. I firmly told them both that I didn't want to get involved again, what happened eighteen years ago was a big mistake which I regret now."

"Instead of killing them both, you could have just walked away?" said Abbot frowning.

"No, it would have been too risky" he said taking another gulp of lukewarm tea.

"So why do you think it would have been hard to walk away?"

"They would have pestered me and hounded me until I gave them what they wanted again. I couldn't have let that happen again" he said crushing his empty cup in anger.

"So, what I don't understand is why two men went in the churchyard, and only one came out talking" she asked frowning.

"Matthew phoned me early one morning whilst I was in the office, he told me he'd recognised me whilst sitting over in the café across the road, I don't know how he even found me, the bank didn't tell anyone where I'd been transferred to."

"And?" asked Peter's still toying with her pen in frustration.

"Well, he must have tracked me down somehow, mustn't he?"

"So how do you think he tracked you down?"

"By chance possibly" he said shrugging his shoulders.

"Ok then, what happened?" Peter's asked scribbling down his answer.

"I made an appointment for him to meet me in Yarmouth churchyard about nine o'clock, I can't remember the exact time, anyway when we were both out of sight from the street and behind the church, that's when I decided to strike him" he said clearing his throat.

"And what did you strike him with?" she asked firmly.

"I'd hidden a baseball bat, inside my jacket and a knife in my pocket."

"But we've got you on your own banks CCTV, we know it's you, because the camera picked up the back of your head, we can just make out from the grainy picture your receding hairline."

"That was the night before, I changed the date and time on the video" the man said confidently.

"But that puts you more in the doo doo, because that would still mean you were the last person to see him alive" said Peter's leaning his elbows on the table.

"I know I just panicked; I didn't know what else to do" he said beginning to fidget in his chair.

"And what excuse did you give Paul to meet you?" she asked sarcastically.

"I told him the same as I told Matthew, to meet me in Yarmouth churchyard, then when we were at the back of the church, I did exactly what I did to Matthew."

"So why did you stab them both, if you struck them with a baseball bat?" asked Peter's taking a sip of cold tea.

"To make sure they were dead of course" he said arrogantly.

"So, you are admitting on tape that you murdered Paul and Matthew Andrews?"

"I am."

"Oh, they were definitely dead alright, you didn't have to pick up the sodding pieces, and what did you do with the baseball bat?" said Abbot angrily.

"I put it in the dustbin behind the bank, I know the dustbin men come early on Monday mornings, I didn't know what else to do, I had my reputation to consider" he said wide eyed.

"You didn't consider thinking about the two brother's reputation, did you?" she said shaking her head.

"I've felt nothing but guilt ever since, I just didn't know any other way to deal with it."

"You could have reported them both to the police, we have a law in this country about blackmail, that would have been the easier option."

"What happens now?" asked the man nervously.

"You'll be charged with the murder of Paul and Matthew Andrews then you'll be taken down to the cells, where you will await a trial date."

"Hopefully, you won't have to wait long" said Peter's finishing off his cold tea.

Sergeant Peter's, could you take Mr Edwards to be charged and then down to the cells for me please?"

"Ok."

"Interview terminated at fifteen thirty hours" she said switching off the tape recorder.

Later in Abbot's office. She sat at her desk deep in

thought as Peter's sat opposite her frowning. They both sat in silence not knowing what the other one was thinking. Abbot's mind was all over the place, not with just the double murders, but with Richard and also Ian. She didn't want Ian to go to the mainland. She thought they still worked well as a team together. As for Richard, she really didn't know what to do, but by the looks of things, he'd certainly found someone new.

"Well, we got our man in the end."

"Yes, we did" she said blankly.

"Ok, there's nothing else keeping me here now, I think I'll go and pack up my desk" he said rising to his feet.

"Right."

"Right" he repeated.

"So, your definitely going?"

"Yes, I think it's best, don't you?" he said shoving his hands in his pockets.

"Well, it's been a pleasure working together" she said raising to her feet.

Abbot walked around her desk and gave him a reassuring smile. She slipped her hair behind her left ear, then reached out her hand, for him to take hold of to shake. He smiled back at her, taking hold of it firmly. He could see a glint in her eyes. Or could it be a tear? She did really have some kind of feelings for Ian, but as they both know, they had to try and keep it professional.

"You know, we made a damn good team, me and you, shame your leaving" she said still holding his hand.

"Yes, well, maybe we were just too good together?" he said with a chuckle.

"Is that what you think?" he said letting go of her hand.

"I don't know what to think anymore Karen" he said opening the door.

He reluctantly wondered over to the door. He pulled down hard on the door handle then opened it wide. He exited her office, slamming the door behind him then walked over to his desk. He reached his own desk, dragging his chair in anger from under his desk. Then he sat down looking in the direction of her office. He knew in his mind how he felt about her. But what and how did she feel about him?

But as a serving detective of many years, who'd worked alongside Abbot for so long he knew what he'd done a few nights back was wrong and unprofessional. He sighed deep into the air.

Later that night Abbot parked her car at the Isle of Wight Pearls car park.

She lit a cigarette standing freezing in the nighttime chill. She blew out a plume of smoke as she stared out at the endless miles of black raging sea that stretched out in front of her. A strong wind was blowing her hair into her face causing her to sweep the messy strands and flicked them behind her ears.

She pulled herself deeper into her thick warm coat. She watched in the distance as the streetlights of silver and gold that danced and flickered in the wind. A number of cars roared past at speed breaking the darkness with the beam of their headlights.

She listened to the sound of the breaking waves that crashed hard against the eroding coastline. She inhaled hard blowing out the last plume of smoke stubbing it out in front of her on the damp ground with her boot.

She opened the car door with some effort from the force of the wind, sliding into the driver's seat. She was about to wrap her seatbelt around her when a familiar car pulled alongside hers. The figure alighted from his car, then walked around his car to hers. She rolled down her window and gave him a reassuring smile.

"And what brings you here Sergerant?"

"You?"

"Ok, and how did you know I'd be here?"

"Oh, you know, just a wild guess" he said leaning in towards her.

"Won't your landlady of bolted the front door by now?" she asked sniggering.

"Maybe!" he said shrugging his shoulders.

"Don't you care?"

"Not anymore."

"Ok, so what do you care about?"

"I care about you."

"Ok, why?"

"I think you know why?" he said stroking her arm.

"Look Ian, we both know that…" she said cutting herself off.

"What?" he asked frowning.

"It wasn't a good idea what we did the other night, it was a big mistake, and we shouldn't have let it happen. I know I shouldn't of, but I let my emotions and vulnerability run away with me. I think its best we leave it where it is, and move on, don't you?" she said turning the key in the ignition.

She rolled up her window then released her handbrake. But before she turned out of the car park, she glanced in her rear-view mirror and watched him standing there for a long second in the glow of his headlights. He ran his hands through his hair in frustration. She indicated right, then drove off into the darkness.

About the Author

I was born in Nuneaton on 22nd November 1971. Many famous writers have come from Warwickshire. William Shakespeare, George Eliot: Novelist Mary Ann Evans, known by her pen name, Ken Loach, the award-winning film and TV Director was also born in Nuneaton. I studied TV & Media Production at North Warwickshire College of Technology and Art in 1992. This is when I started writing about my main character in screenplay form, but unfortunately didn't get any of my project work commissioned by any TV companies. So, I started writing in book form. I have always had a curiosity in crime, such as Agatha Christie, and Colin Dexter.

It was like having a conversation with myself; working my way through whatever problems were bothering me at that time. At the time, I was struggling in lots of ways. I would write for hours, just pouring whatever was in my mind, onto the paper in front of me. I can release my emotions through the pen. I go on a journey and see where my mind takes me.

I feel my writing has got better as I progressed through the "Dead" series. I write a lot of plots and ideas when I am out and about in my notebooks. I jot down ideas I have floating around in my head. I started visiting places, such as (country lanes, listening to the sound of the sea, and feeling the wind and rain against my face, to feel the moment of the character(s) whilst feeling the emotions of the characters in my books. Setting the scene and feeling immersed in what I was writing. I can then pick and choose my ideas and the understanding of the character(s) as the mood takes me. I use my surroundings and senses to make my writing feel more real. I then apply and develop these ideas into my books, it is a satisfying feeling. It is a way of me expressing myself in a calm, and clear way through the journey of the writing and the character(s). This gives me a sense of achievement.

My crime fiction and murder mysteries include the "Dead" series of ten novels. In 2019, I started writing my first novel "Dead Quiet", which is the first in the series of ten books. Once I had written my first book, I decided I wanted to continue with a second, and a third, and so on, now I am on my tenth book. I have enjoyed this journey of writing a series of books, which has certainly become a big part of my life now.

I think my books have interesting themes and I want the reader to think so too. I feel I write very well for a beginner. When editors, publishers (and, ultimately readers) read my books. I want the reader to feel that they cannot get enough of the "Dead" series. And I want the reader(s) to develop some kind of love or hate relationship with the character(s). And that's the kind of feeling I would love with my audience. Great writing, plus great ideas and plots will work just fine every time. As a person I am no academic, but I write really well, and I think that people will love my material, and the twists and turns in my books.